COURAGE OF THE CONQUERED

BOOK THREE OF THE RAITHLINDRATH SERIES

Robert Ryan

Cover Design by www.ebooklaunch.com

ISBN-13 978-0-9942054-0-7
(print edition)

Trotting Fox Press

I0458070

Contents

1. Old Enemies

Emotions washed over Lanrik. They tightened his chest, constricted his throat and brought a film of tears to his eyes. Yet they were of a kind so peculiar, so seldom felt, that he could not name them.

He remained perfectly still, but his gaze leaped like a living thing over the miles between the hill on which he stood and the city below.

Esgallien. His old home. The place that would always be home no matter where he roamed, even if he lived as long as Aranloth.

Not that he would. He was not sure that he wanted to, either. For what he felt now must only be a shadow, a token, of what such a life entailed.

The city gleamed like a raindrop caught by the midsummer sun and turned by its bright rays into a brilliant diamond. But the city, just like the raindrop, was ephemeral. Nothing lasted forever, and he knew with sudden insight that the forces of chaos gnawed at the great just the same as the small.

The splendor of the city held his gaze, but he was not unaware of the flocks of crows that hopped and fluttered over refuse, or of the sluggish layer of smoke, spewed from countless fireplaces, that hovered cloudlike above the sprawl of buildings. It was just that his heart was drawn to what was good. And there was much of that in an ancient city founded by a hardworking and talented people.

Esgallien had not changed since he had left. At least, not from this distance. Yet for all its grandeur, its many

3

bridges, its tall buildings, its green parks and massive squares, it seemed smaller to him. And even more precious.

His old self, a Raithlin in service to the king, had enjoyed living there. Now, he was exiled. The city seemed peaceful, and yet every tale coming from it told a story of woe and turmoil. It seemed strong, even invincible, but it had never been at greater risk from its enemies, which were many.

He sighed. The city's towers pierced the air, their lofty roofs glinted in the sun, but there were shadow-filled alleys below. The palace gleamed, noble and fair, and yet he knew what greed and corruption dwelt inside. The Red Cloth of Victory fluttered from its tallest flagpole. It represented the heart of Esgallien society: courage, determination, loyalty. It was a reminder of Conhain's sacrifice on founding the city. But those who ruled beneath it dishonored his name.

His old self would not have seen these things. But he did. The city had not changed – *he* had.

A breeze tugged at the banner, and it attracted his attention. It was not the original cloth, of course. It was merely a flag, dyed a bright shade of crimson, not the one soaked with Conhain's blood. No one knew where that was. It must have turned to dust centuries ago. So much of the past was gone, but the spirit of the city founders was still alive. Ebona could not break it in a matter of months, or even years. Of that, he was certain.

Nevertheless, Conhain's famous quote ran through his mind. *Nothing lasts forever. Not men, nor chiefs … nor even cities.*

Lanrik had seen enough, lived long enough now, to feel the truth of that statement. And to fear that it might come to pass during his lifetime.

Aranloth's horse swished its tail and stamped a hoof. The sudden movement drew Lanrik out of his pensive mood.

"They're down there somewhere," he said. "The Raithlin and the Lindrath. Alive or dead. And who knows what they've endured since Ebona entered the city."

Aranloth closed his eyes. When he opened them, he looked away from Esgallien.

"She'll have persecuted them. There was more than one report that she was trying to hunt them all down. I believed it. But your old friends are resourceful. She'll not have had everything her own way."

"Lots of rumors reached Lòrenta," Lanrik said. "Most of them contradicted each other. I can't help wonder if even one of the Raithlin is left though, still less the Lindrath. I've lost count of the supposed instances of imprisonment and escape. But torture and death are more likely."

Erlissa placed an arm around his shoulders. "We'll find out what happened, Lan."

He leaned in toward her. "If he's alive, we might even be able to help," he said. "But one way or another, I intend to discover the truth."

He looked over at the Lòhren. "Are you sure you can't come with us?"

"I would if I could," Aranloth answered. "But my own task is as necessary as yours, albeit in a different way." He patted his robes where he kept a pouch filled with the seeds the Guardian had given him. "I promised Carnona I'd plant these in the Graèglin Dennath. It was our bargain when I needed her help, and I must keep to that promise, even if that help is no longer needed."

Lanrik wondered if that was all there was to it. It seemed to him that the lòhren had other business. He

5

always kept secrets, even if he did so for a good purpose, and Lanrik was getting better at telling when that was so.

"Then we'll just have to get by without you," he said with resignation.

Aranloth held his gaze. "You'll scrape through, I think." He glanced at Erlissa. "But the two of you must stick together. Whatever you do, don't get separated. You have no friends down there except yourselves. I've been in places like this before. Fear, spite and malice thrive. You cannot trust anybody, no matter how much you want to. And remember, try not to interfere in anything. That'll only draw attention to you. What we need is reliable information about what's happening. Only then can we decide how to deal with Ebona." He paused for a moment, seeking to draw some last bit of advice from the well of his experience. "Stay out of harm's way. Listen and learn. Keep your mouths closed and your ears open – that's the way to get through this."

Aranloth held out his hand, and Lanrik shook it firmly. When he let go, Erlissa reached up to give the lòhren a hug. Aranloth seemed taken aback by that. He looked for a moment like he wished to stay, but then he nudged his horse forward and turned to the right. His path was around the city, and then on toward Esgallien Ford.

"Remember," he said over his shoulder. "Tonight is a full moon. We'll meet at the next one on the tor."

Erlissa ignored his comment. "Be careful," she said.

Lanrik had no wish to part from the lòhren, or to see him go into danger by himself. Still less did he want to go to the tor again. Lathmai's suffering gave him nightmares even now, and seeing the place where she died would only freshen bad memories. On the other hand, her grave should not remain untended, and the tor was the logical place to meet. It was easily located, and it

6

offered a clear view for many leagues. With all the enemies they had, that was a necessary precaution.

Neither he nor Erlissa spoke while the lòhren guided his mount between rocks and shrubs along a faint trail into the wilderness. Lanrik was not sure about her, but he felt his stomach sink. Aranloth had helped them through many dangerous times, and now he had to leave when they faced a new one. They should be safe from the witch if they followed his advice, but even carefully crafted plans faltered in the face of the unexpected.

When the lòhren disappeared into a thicket of scrubby trees, they looked once more at the city.

"Time for us to go as well," Erlissa said.

By way of answer Lanrik started down the road. They walked in a comfortable silence. And if the lòhren was not with them, they had each other.

Lanrik fingered the silver ring that he wore. Aranloth had given it to him, and Erlissa wore one just like it. It was a ward against Ebona. It would offer no help if the witch attacked them, but it would conceal them from her probing mind should she have cause to seek them out. Not that she had any reason to suspect their entry into the city, but it did not pay to underestimate her, or those in her service. She hated the two of them. They had each thwarted and disdained her, and her reserves of forgiveness were low, while her capacity for revenge was high. After all, she had held a grudge against Aranloth for a thousand years.

He glanced over at Erlissa. For a moment he studied her, and then he smiled.

She frowned. "What's so amusing?"

"You look different … as a blonde."

She ran a hand through her hair. "I don't think it suits me. I only hope all the trouble that Aranloth took to dye it was worthwhile."

Lanrik grew serious. "I think it was," he said. "The Royal Guard are sure to have our descriptions, and Ebona will also have informants throughout the city. If I'm having trouble recognizing you, I don't see how they could."

She returned his appraising glance. "You look different too, you know."

He grew uncomfortable. "I look stupid with black hair instead of brown."

"No," she said. "It suits you, but that's not what I meant."

"What *did* you mean?"

"You look really odd without your Raithlin clothes."

He shrugged. "If I *look* odd, I assure you, I feel even stranger."

He had swapped his normal garb, clothes that would have ensured his arrest on sight, for a plain pair of tan trousers and a wine-red tunic so faded by wear as to be near colorless. But he had not chosen the clothes without due thought. Not only would their drabness allow him to appear unremarkable in a crowd, but if he had to hide, those colors would blend well with bricks and tiles.

To further their disguises Lanrik carried Erlissa's walnut staff. He also wore a sword. Although it was a Raithlin blade, etched with the trotting fox motif, he refused to leave it behind. It was an act of defiance against Ebona and King Murhain. Futile, perhaps, but it made him feel better. Anyway, he should not have any cause to draw it, so no one would ever know. At least, he hoped so. It felt a suddenly foolish decision the closer he came to the city though.

He carried the staff lightly as he walked. It felt cool to his touch, and heavy, even for walnut. Not only did his carrying it, instead of her, reduce the chance that someone would recognize her as a lòhren, it served another important purpose. Part of his disguise was to act as a bodyguard to her pretense as a healer. Bodyguards often carried staffs and used their blades only as a last line of defense.

They walked easily but quickly down the hill. Their horses were on their way back to Lòrenta with several of the new Raithlin who had come this far, but no more, as a training exercise.

Ahead, at the base of the hill where a creek ran between steep banks, was their first stop: Bridge Inn. The bridge after which it was named spanned the banks.

While they made their way toward it, Lanrik kept a close eye on the countryside. And though the road looked exactly as it normally did: well made, turfed and slightly raised in the middle to drain water, the countryside did not.

All about him he saw indications that something was amiss. The farms were quiet, and there were no laborers in sight. The villa doors were closed, when normally they were open. If they were not open, at least some of the side doors were usually kept ajar for the ease of workers that came and went with great frequency.

The fields seemed unnaturally still, except for the few horses that he could see. There were no men hoeing weeds, mending fences or spreading manure. Most of all, he noticed that many paddocks that needed ploughing remained untilled and thick with weeds. That disturbed him most of all, for this was a prosperous area, home to the many studs that bred horses for the races in the Haranast. The problems he saw spoke of ongoing neglect and little hope for the future.

Erlissa sensed it as well. She looked about her carefully, her gaze lingering most on the closed villas. But they said nothing to each other as they walked. They kept their eyes wide open and alert, and glanced frequently toward the city beyond the inn that must lie under the same dread or burden that sucked the life out of the land.

At length, they came to the bridge. It was old, of pitted and weathered stone, built in the early days of the kingdom. For all of that, it was solid and secure. It had survived many floods, and so too had the inn beside it. That was Lanrik's first choice of a place to gather information, for nowhere was there more news to be had than where food filled bellies and beer loosened tongues.

He remembered with fondness the many occasions that he had drunk the beer of the inn. It was at times a haunt for Raithlin. Especially in the early stages of training, for some of the most experienced instructors lived in this quarter of the city. But his training days were well in the past, and no one would likely recognize him now, even without a disguise, except another Raithlin. And if he met one of them, he would be more than happy.

He remembered the stories that he had heard here, of how Rhodmai, who had once poured beer for weary travelers as a barmaid, had become Queen of Esgallien and ruled in her own right after the king's death. She had lived to one hundred and one, and folklore alleged that she attributed her longevity to a glass of beer every day. It was a popular inn, and he hoped that in its crowded taproom he would hear much news without even having to ask questions.

They slowed as they crossed the bridge. Below, water gurgled in the creek, but it was not as it once was. Discarded rubbish lay washed up on the banks, or had been thrown over the side of the stone rails, and the corpse of a small animal, bloated and stinking, floated down the current.

There were now several people moving about, probably travelers between villas or workers returning from the Haranast to the horse studs. Some carried sacks over their shoulder, but they all walked hurriedly, whatever their destination. With a jolt, Lanrik realized that some of them might even be refugees seeking escape from the city.

All of them kept their hoods up and their heads down. They did not speak to each other, still less to him and Erlissa who were heading toward the city. There were no friendly greetings, not even a nod or a wave as was customary on Esgallien's open roads. And when he caught a glimpse of their faces, he saw nothing but signs of woe and fear.

"It's worse that we thought," Erlissa whispered to him.

He had no answer to that. He was expecting it to be bad, but a sense of dread was coming to life the closer they came to the inn, and he wondered what the rest of the city would be like when they reached it.

Instinctively, he moved closer to Erlissa. "They're like a conquered people," he said.

"It's as if they're beyond hope."

Lanrik did not think that was the case. He felt that regardless of their appearance, under the right circumstances, they would fight back. Murhain and Ebona would not have everything their own way. Not for much longer, anyway. Once he and Erlissa discovered the truth of how things stood, Aranloth would devise a plan to defeat the witch.

They reached the inn and stood quietly for a moment before the door. It was closed, a thing that Lanrik had never seen before except in winter. And even then only on the coldest days when a wind blew from the north.

He glanced at the sign near the door. It hung neatly from a chain, but it creaked and rattled in a way that was lonesome. Bridge Inn, it declared, but the writing was small. Far larger was the portrait of Rhodmai, an old lady seated in a comfortable chair, with a mug in her hands and a twinkle in her eye. Her image was reassuring at least.

He placed a hand on the door and opened it. What he saw as it swung on rusted hinges was something so unexpected that it drained the reassurance right from him. Standing on the other side, scrutinizing him closely, were two Royal Guards. Beyond, he saw several others in the same uniform. Each of them eyed him carefully.

2. A Dangerous Path

Lanrik forced a smile.

"Hello," he said. Despite his cheery tone, his first reaction had been to raise the staff in a defensive position. He had covered it by pretending it was a kind of wave, but was not sure if that had worked.

Neither of the Royal Guards bothered to acknowledge his greeting. Instead, they looked at him coldly.

"Name and occupation," the closer of the two said. His tone was that of a bored man doing a distasteful job.

Lanrik resisted the urge to show offense at the rudeness. Instead, he offered the story he and Erlissa had prepared.

"I'm Marik. I serve as a bodyguard."

The soldier eyed him as though he doubted his competence for the role. "And who needs *your* protection?"

Lanrik gestured behind him. "Tamril is a healer."

Erlissa stepped forward and gave a slight curtsey.

The second guard leaned over a nearby table and wrote on a sheet of tattered parchment. When he was done, the two of them did not bother to say anything further but returned to their seats near a curtained window. Evidently, they kept a lookout for travelers. But Lanrik was intrigued. For whom did they watch?

What he wanted to do most of all was get out of the room. But to leave now would only draw suspicion. Instead, he ushered Erlissa through and closed the door behind him. They must go inside and stay long enough for at least one drink.

The room was near empty of customers, but there was no lack of Royal Guards. There must have been a dozen, and Lanrik doubted they were there for leisure. They were stationed here for a reason; and that must be to look for someone, and someone expected to give them trouble, or there would not be so many.

He saw a free table against the left wall and walked over to it. His boots clanked loudly on the wooden floor, for there was little conversation among the guards and the room was quiet.

The tables and chairs were of oak, solid and thick, as was the long bar that ran the length of the furthest wall. His chosen spot was near a hearth, but it was cold, and it looked like no fire had burned within it for some time. Above the mantel was another image of Rhodmai. She beamed down at them merrily, and Lanrik wondered what she would have thought of the way travelers had come to be treated at her inn.

After a moment, a serving maid approached. She was young, nervous and kept her gaze fixed firmly on the floor as though determined to do her job properly and to stay out of trouble.

"What can I get you?" she asked.

"I'll have a beer," Lanrik answered.

The girl turned to Erlissa.

"I'll have the same."

"Anything to eat?"

Lanrik hesitated. He wanted to get out of here, but it might still be a good place to obtain information, and he did not want to arouse suspicion.

"What sort of stew do you have today?"

"It's mutton this week."

It was not Lanrik's favorite, but he was growing hungry.

"A bowl of that and some bread," he said.

"There's no bread today," she replied. He caught a hint of emotion in her voice. She liked her current situation little better than he did. The guards must have given her a hard time.

"The stew will be fine by itself."

"I'll have it too," Erlissa added.

When the girl returned with the drinks, Lanrik took a slow sip. The beer tasted watery, far from the good brew that he was accustomed to here.

He took a deeper drink and casually looked around. There were a handful of other patrons, more than he had at first thought, for they were tucked away in nooks and corners just like the one he had chosen near the hearth. They were hushed, and there was none of the normal sounds of laughter and loud talk that usually filled inns.

He studied the others carefully. They appeared to be hard men, laborers of some kind. Their clothes were wrinkled and coarse, their hands darkened by dirt and years of toil, but they drank with a certain reserved grace, lowering their mugs with care so as not to make a noise or spill any of the contents. He guessed that they probably worked at nearby horse studs.

Leaning up against the bar was a huddle of three men. They were younger, lank haired and surly. They were not guards, and Lanrik doubted that they were laborers. He could not tell their trades, but knew instinctively that he did not like them. They were dressed too poorly to be nobles, and yet well enough for him to be suspicious of their source of income.

These men were louder than the other patrons, and though they did not carry swords, he was sure that he saw the telltale bulge of knife handles beneath their tunics. From time to time they cast leering looks at Erlissa. That she ignored their attention seemed to upset them.

Lanrik and Erlissa did not speak much. They sipped their drinks and kept an eye on those around them.

When their stew arrived, the girl placed it before them carefully on the pitted oak table and gave them spoons, and for the first time, a slight smile.

Lanrik thanked her, and her expression brightened further. He had a feeling that good manners were scarce at the inn lately and that she appreciated it.

The stew was surprisingly good. At least, it seemed that way after the weeks on the road that it had taken to reach Esgallien. But it was not as good as what the captain of the Royal Guard ate. He sat at the head of a table in the middle of the room, surrounded by his men, but he received a much grander meal. It looked to be the same stew, only he was given bread, fruit and cheese with it.

Lanrik and Erlissa ate with relish. When they were done, and their bowls cleared, he noticed the captain gazing at him darkly. He was about to look away, not wanting contact of any sort between them, but the man gestured curtly for him to come over. It was a haughty flick of the hand, and Lanrik fought hard to suppress his anger. But he endured it, as doubtless many others had done in Esgallien since the witch had entered the city. The Royal Guard had always tended toward arrogance, but under her influence the worst of them seemed to feel empowered.

Lanrik gave Erlissa a quick look of warning and then approached the captain's table.

"May I be of assistance, Sir?" Lanrik asked.

The other man took a swig of his beer before he answered.

"Don't call me Sir. My rank is captain. Captain Brinhain, and that is how you will address me."

Lanrik had known the correct form of address, but as a supposed traveler from other parts of Alithoras it was better not to show familiarity with the city's customs. He suppressed a smile though: that it irked the other man was satisfying.

Brinhain flicked his glance to Erlissa, and then back to him.

"I'm told that your companion is a healer."

Lanrik nodded. "Yes." It was a curt answer, but he guessed where this was going and did not want to encourage it.

"Is she any good? Or is she a fraud like most others?"

"She's quite good," Lanrik said. "I've seen her work many cures, but of course, not everyone responds to treatment."

"Call her over."

Lanrik thought that hardly necessary, as the captain had talked through the whole conversation loud enough for everyone in the room to hear. Nor did he want to, but there was no choice.

He turned and looked straight at Erlissa. He read uncertainty in her eyes, but also an understanding that their ruse had not been discovered and that she must go along with things to keep it that way.

She approached the table and gave one of her elegant curtseys.

"Captain Brinhain," she said. Her smile was sweet, as though she had not heard any of the captain's insults, though everyone knew she must have. Lanrik wished that he could better hide his own chagrin, but then he realized that her very politeness served as a subtle rebuke.

Brinhain was oblivious to it. He lifted his foot up and rested it gently on the table. The boot was off, and the bare foot seemed red and swollen, especially around the joint of the big toe.

"My foot hurts," he said. "What can be done to cure it?"

Erlissa did not hesitate. She looked at his foot closely, and gingerly touched the big toe as though feeling for heat.

After a moment she looked up at him. "You have the gout, Captain. It's a disease that chiefly affects the foot, but sometimes the knees and elbows as well. Do you have pain in those areas too?"

"No," he said impatiently. "I already know it's the gout – I want to know the cure."

"Of course," Erlissa said, as though she was completely oblivious to the fact that he was being difficult.

She cast her gaze over the table and the remains of the meal that the captain had eaten.

"The gout is a condition that usually responds to a change in diet. If you restrict your intake of rich foods, and especially of beer, you'll notice an improvement. Perhaps even a large one."

The captain looked at her with hard eyes and shook his head. Slowly, he placed his foot back on the ground, though Lanrik noticed that he did not put much weight on it.

"I asked for a cure," the man said, "not a lifetime sentence of deprivation."

What happened next took everybody by surprise. The captain lashed out, slapping Erlissa across the face. She staggered back a few steps, and then looked at him with blazing eyes.

Lanrik felt a cold fury rise inside him. He wanted to drop the staff and draw his sword, but instead he merely stepped between them. He knew that he was in range of the captain, should Brinhain wish to strike him as well. It was a gesture of defiance, one that almost taunted the captain to react, and part of Lanrik wished that he would, for then the response would be swift and sure, and damn the consequences.

The captain must have read something of that in his eyes. Perhaps he feared what might be done to him before his men could intervene. For whatever reason, he chose only to give an indifferent flick of his fingers.

"Dismissed," he said.

Lanrik did not move. After a moment, he spoke in a soft but distinct voice.

"That will be five coppers."

The captain's face went white. Lanrik could see him tremble with indignation, and yet a consultation had taken place and a diagnosis given. The man owed the money, and a failure to pay would make him look bad, even if he could get away with it. All eyes were on him. Or, Lanrik thought reluctantly, on himself. He could have done without that, and without making an enemy of this man, and yet he must also uphold the role that he played as a bodyguard. It was his job to ensure payment for services rendered, and it would seem strange if he did not try.

The captain, now bright red, pulled a wallet from his tunic. Slowly, he counted out the coins and then cast them onto the table.

Lanrik placed his hands over them swiftly, but without seeming haste, and stopped them before they skidded to the floor.

He pocketed the coins and guided Erlissa back to their table.

The captain called over to them after they had sat down.

"It's getting late in the day. I assume you'll be staying here for the night, so I'll require your services again in the morning."

Lanrik did not want to stay overnight. And yet he could think of no reason to turn down work.

Erlissa exchanged a glance with him before she answered.

"I'll be here, Captain."

They ordered more beers, and the afternoon passed swiftly. Now, a small but steady flow of patrons came through the door. They showed no liking for the recording of their names on the parchment, but whether by long habit of attending the inn or by virtue of its reputation, that did not stop them from entering.

For the most part, the newcomers were farm hands. They did not speak to the guards, nor the guards to them, and they soon found tables and talked quietly among themselves.

Lanrik sipped at his beer and spent most of the time listening. Much of the conversation around him turned on the weather; a subject that farmers and Raithlin often had in common, and one that many other people rarely saw the use of. If it rained, they stayed indoors. But farmers and Raithlin had a different perspective. To them, it was a blessing or a curse depending on the situation – but it was a thing to which they were never indifferent.

He caught Erlissa's glance when one group started to talk about events in the city. This was not a safe topic within earshot of the guards, and it died down as swiftly as it began. Lanrik strained to hear while it lasted, but the men said nothing that he had not already guessed: the city was in turmoil, food was ever more expensive and jobs fewer.

The inn grew dark, and the serving maid lit several candles. It was a feeble effort against the growing night, but it seemed that candles were as scarce here as goodwill.

The door opened soon after, and a young man endured the same routine that everyone else had. He was obviously another farm hand, and it looked as though he had been drinking elsewhere before coming to the Bridge Inn.

The guards let him through with little fuss, seeming to know him or at least to recognize him as a local. He was tall, but very young, and Lanrik watched him closely. The man swayed ever so slightly, and no doubt beer had loosened his tongue as much as it put a falter in his steps.

Lanrik had a feeling that trouble was coming. But when it came, it came swiftly and did not take the form that he expected.

The newcomer looked around him, as though trying to identify anybody he knew. Failing to see any familiar faces, he set himself and started to walk to the bar. Halfway between the door and his destination, he paused. Blinking at the candles, he muttered something unintelligible, and then spoke in a suddenly loud voice.

"It's so dark in here that you'd need the tracking skills of a Raithlin to find the bar."

The inn went dead still, and the young man looked around in bafflement.

"Was it something I said?"

The guards turned on him. One of them struck him hard in the face and another kicked him when he fell down.

"The Raithlin are dead!" the first guard shouted. "Every last one of them, and good riddance. Their name isn't spoken anymore. Do you understand?"

The second guard kicked him again to emphasize the point.

The youth struggled to a sitting position. Blood streamed from a gash on his cheek, and he winced as he breathed as though one of his ribs was broken, which Lanrik thought might well be the case.

The youth looked around him, suddenly sober. "The Raithlin are all dead," he said. "Sorry, my mistake."

With as much dignity as he could find, the man rose on unsteady legs and staggered out the door.

Lanrik felt sorry for him. He had taken quite a beating, and the pain would be worse when the alcohol wore off. His pity was crowded out by another feeling though. *The Raithlin were dead. All of them.* He felt cold to his very bones, and though it was an outcome that he had earlier feared, to actually hear it stated as a fact was still a shock.

Erlissa reached out and gently placed a hand over his own.

Talk slowly returned to the room, but Lanrik remained still. He only moved when a man at the table adjoining them, quiet and aloof until then, leaned over and whispered.

"It's not so," the man said. "I heard that they escaped the city."

Lanrik tried to hide his excitement. He leaned casually toward the man and whispered back.

"Where did you here that?"

"I heard it said in the Merenloth the day before yesterday – from Bragga Mor himself."

The stranger looked away then, fearful that their conversation might be overheard, but he had said enough.

Lanrik considered the information. He knew Bragga Mor, at least by reputation. He was a famous poet, and he had listened to him perform many times in the Merenloth. He was also a man of wealth and prestige in the city. Where most of his poet friends struggled to earn a living, Bragga Mor had somehow amassed a fortune. It was also said that he spent money as quickly as he received it, mostly on horse betting, drinking and womanizing.

That the man had many contacts in the city was well known. He walked in all circles of Esgallien society, and he was respected, despite his rumored shortcomings. Lanrik remembered that the Lindrath spoke well of him, and that was good enough for him.

He glanced at Erlissa. She read his intent clearly, and gave a nod of agreement. Their next stop must be the Merenloth, and a conversation with the poet to discover what he knew. But first, they must get through the rest of the night at the inn and be rid of Brinhain as soon as possible in the morning.

It soon grew very quiet. The beating had subdued whatever faint spirit of levity that had begun to build, and the small groups of farmhands that had shown up during the afternoon left in quick succession.

Lanrik and Erlissa retired to the upstairs level of the inn as soon as they could. They paused in the hallway outside the room they had secured from the serving maid and spoke for the first time without fear of being overheard.

"Do you think it's true?" Erlissa asked.

Lanrik chewed on his lip. "I *want* it to be true, but we'll only know when we see Bragga Mor. It could be just another wild rumor, but maybe we've discovered a trail to follow."

Erlissa hugged him. "We'll find out, Lan. That's what we came here for. And as we do, we'll learn more about Ebona."

Lanrik gave her a direct look. "It might be harder than we thought. I don't like the attitude of the guards. It seems to me that they think they can get away with anything."

Erlissa nodded. "I know what you mean. Their attitude shows that they *have* been getting away with everything. They were always arrogant, but what I saw tonight makes me wonder if there's any law at all in the city."

"The king has much to answer for," Lanrik said. "The guards were always his, and if they're doing what they like – it's because he's doing what *he* likes."

Erlissa frowned. "Where does their loyalty lie, though?"

"What do you mean?"

"I mean, have they remained faithful to the king, or do they now serve Ebona?"

Lanrik had not considered that before. The king might have become little more than a figurehead. Ebona was the true power, and she would be ordering things to her will. The Royal Guard would have realized that sooner than the rest of the city. Were they all like the ones that he had seen today? Had they thrown their lot in with her and sought to ride to ever-greater power under her influence? Or were there some that refuted her? It was something he had to try to find out, because it might make a difference when Aranloth moved to overthrow the witch.

Erlissa opened the door to the room, but Lanrik hesitated.

24

"What's the matter?"

He grinned at her. "Don't you know?"

"Know what?"

"Bodyguards sleep outside the door of their employer's room. That way they can ensure no one gets inside."

Erlissa shrugged. "I don't think anybody would notice, except me."

Lanrik shook his head. "They'll notice. We've already got off on the wrong foot with Brinhain. We can't afford to arouse any suspicion."

Erlissa stamped her foot. "How can you sleep on hard timber?"

"I'm a Raithlin. I can sleep anywhere."

Erlissa pursed her lips and shook her head as though she could not believe what she was hearing.

"At least let me get you a pillow."

"Just a blanket will be fine," he said. "Bodyguards aren't supposed to use pillows. It encourages too deep a sleep."

"How do you know so much about bodyguards?"

"I spent a fair amount of time at inns when I was training. Retired Raithlin often act as instructors, and we moved around to different parts of the city depending on which instructor we had to see."

Erlissa went inside, obviously still unconvinced that it was necessary to maintain their ruse so strictly. She returned after a moment with a thick blanket and handed it to him.

"That should keep you warm," she said. "But it's going to be a long night."

"The sooner it's over, and tomorrow's consultation with Brinhain, the better."

They said goodnight, and Erlissa closed the door. Lanrik listened as she prepared for bed. When the noise stopped, and he knew she would need nothing else, he sat down, leaned his back against the door and closed his eyes.

But he did not sleep. There was truth in the comment that bodyguards were not supposed to use pillows. The hard floor made anything but dozing impossible, and that suited him tonight. He did not like Brinhain, his guards, or for that matter anybody else staying at the inn. He trusted them even less, and he intended to be prepared for anything.

The night wore on. He dozed fitfully, rarely sleeping for more than a few minutes at a time. And yet it was restful anyway. He did not need much sleep, and a few minutes here and there were sufficient to see him well enough rested for the next morning.

As the night drifted by he thought of what he had learned so far. It was still all rumor, but at least he and Erlissa had seen things with their own eyes. They would learn more tomorrow, hopefully from Bragga Mor, but also just by moving through the city.

No matter how bad the influence of the Witch-queen, people must still leave their homes for work and food. The markets would attract people, and that was a place to observe them and see how things stood. It was also a good place to see what the Royal Guard were doing. Were they concentrated on places like this, places where outsiders often stopped on their way to the city? Or were they spread out among Esgallien's population? That alone would serve to indicate who Ebona feared most. And knowing that was a guide to how she might best be opposed.

The noise had long ceased from the common room below, and what few patrons that had stayed, as well as the guards, were now in their beds. As the night wore on, Lanrik felt less inclined to sleep. He had rested well, and now he simply sat against the door and dozed. His hands, beneath the warm blanket, rested loosely on the cold timber of Erlissa's staff.

The hours slipped by in half wakefulness, and away in the city he heard the intermittent barking of dogs, and eventually the crowing of a rooster. The night wore on until dawn was near, that hour when sleep was often deepest. But Lanrik remained alert, and it was then that his instincts jerked his eyes open.

He did not know what had roused him. He sat there, unmoving but wide-awake, and his heart thrummed in his chest as though he was running a one-mile race.

Nothing happened. The light from the moon filtered through the narrow window at the end of the hallway and filled the passage with a river of pale light. And then he heard a creak followed by a faint rasp. At the end of the hall, where the stairs descended into the common room, shadows thickened. After a few moments they took the shape of three menacing figures: men who paused on the landing; men who watched, waited and checked to see if he was awake.

He was more than awake. His heart thudded even faster now, and a cold sweat beaded his skin; but he made no move. He wanted to see what the men would do. Perhaps they would be scared off if he stood. Or perhaps not. They might attack anyway, trying to rob him and Erlissa, and then make a quick escape. And if he let them know that he saw them, he would lose the advantage of surprise. And he needed that, for if there was a fight it would be three against one.

The rooster crowed again, long and shrill, and at that moment the men began to steal toward him. He knew them now, dim shapes though they were: the three surly men from the common room who had leered at Erlissa, and he feared they had more on their minds than robbery.

He gripped the cold wood of Erlissa's staff. His sword would have been better, but the staff was ready to hand, and it was a dangerous weapon in its own right. It gave an advantage of reach, which would be welcome, for though these men had not worn swords they certainly carried knives.

They swept as slow shadows down the hall and approached. He caught the glint of steel on drawn blades, saw even the grim cast of their faces, and knew that they had come for murder.

Anger boiled in his blood, and his chest beat no longer to the thrum of fear, but to a rage that burned fiercer than any fire.

He flung the blanket at the nearest man and leaped to his feet. The staff speared through the shadowy air, its dark walnut nearly invisible, and its tip drove like a dagger thrust into the groin of the second nearest man. There was a cry of pain, loud and sharp, and the assailant reeled away in agony.

The third man jumped in, knife flashing. Lanrik felt a whoosh of air near his face as he dodged to the side. The blade missed him, but the man's arm bunted into his neck. Lanrik charged, shouldering his attacker and sending him crashing into the opposite wall. As the man bounced off it, Lanrik smashed the staff's tip into his head and knocked him out.

The other two men rounded on him. They had not seen a staff wielded like this before, and it confused them. They were used to both ends being used equally, not the one tip like a spear point. Few knew the technique, for it was something that Lanrik's uncle had taught him, and even the Raithlin had only seen it rarely.

His attackers were wary of him, and paused for a moment, but the momentum of their ill will carried them on. They charged together. Lanrik drove the staff point into the first man's chest. There was a crack, perhaps of bone, and he collapsed.

Lanrik ducked under the other man's slash, and now, too close to use the staff properly, he brought his elbow up into the man's groin. The dark figure reeled back, and Lanrik followed him, the tip of the staff poking, stabbing and driving into flesh and bone. The man screamed and fell.

Lanrik stood back. The three men lay on the floor, one unconscious, the other two badly injured. They would not escape the inn.

All around him he became aware of noise. Doors slammed shut, others opened and wide-eyed faces poked out.

Suddenly, the serving maid was there. She was a slim shadow in a white nightgown, pale as the moonlight, but he recognized her.

"What happened?" she asked, staring at the men on the floor.

"They attacked me." He pointed with the staff at Erlissa's door, which opened at that moment. "But I don't think robbery was all that they had in mind."

The girl looked from Erlissa's face to the men. There was no pity in her expression.

"They seemed a bad bunch from the moment they came in," she said, "but the captain is going to have words with you anyway. There's a lot of talk at the moment about banning weapons, and the last time there was a fight he confiscated the man's sword."

Lanrik and Erlissa exchanged glances. Neither of them was prepared to accept that.

"Why is the captain even here?" Lanrik asked.

"He's looking for Raithlin," the girl said. "Apparently, they used to come here sometimes, but it must have been before I started."

Lanrik thought quickly. This was no place to be. He and Erlissa must leave the inn, and they must leave it now.

At that moment, boots clattered on the stairs. Heavy boots, and many of them.

It could only be the guards. Lanrik thanked the girl quickly, went into the room with Erlissa, and shut the door.

Behind them, in the hall, the boots sounded loud and he tried desperately to think of something to do. There were too many men to fight. That was a sure way to get captured or killed. He looked around the room frantically, but he could see no alternative.

3. The Beating Heart

Lanrik put his back to the door and thought. It was locked, but the simple bolt would not withstand any force.

He heard the shuffle of boots and some muted questions on the other side. The injured men would hold the attention of the guards for mere moments, and then they would want to talk to him.

His gaze swept the room, but he saw no way out except the window. He dismissed that immediately as they were on the second story.

Urgent knocking rang against the door.

"Open up!"

It was Brinhain, and Lanrik knew their time was nearly up.

Erlissa straightened, and then called out in a voice with the perfect blend of obedience and vexation at the circumstances.

"Just a moment, Captain! I'm getting dressed."

She was already dressed. All she had done since Lanrik entered the room was swiftly pull on her boots, but her deception would buy them a few more moments. And Lanrik was beginning to get an idea.

He strode to the window, careful not to make noise and give Brinhain the impression that something was going on.

He found the window fastened shut. The latch was stiff, but he jiggled it until it loosened and pushed it open with a creak.

He looked down. It was still dark, but in the predawn gray he could make out enough. It was a long drop; too long to be sure of jumping safely. The last thing either of them could afford was an injury. They could not hope to escape if they could not run, nor could they fight properly if they were already hurt. Not that there was any chance of overcoming so many guards.

And yet he saw something that gave him hope. There was a knee-high mound below the window. A strong smell of manure and straw rose up to him. It ought not to be there, for the stables should have been cleaned every day and the muck carted out to enrich nearby fields, but the neglect that he saw inside the inn obviously extended to the outside.

Beyond the mound was the long and low building that served as the stables. He had been in them before, and there were always horses there. If that was the case now he could not be sure, for the inn was much less busy than it should be. Yet if there were few travelers, there were at least many guards, and there was a fair chance that they had ridden here from their barracks near the palace. He hoped so.

The banging on the door commenced again.

"Open up!" the captain shouted.

"Nearly ready," Erlissa replied.

Lanrik raced to the bed. He picked up the mattress, including all the bedclothes, and carried it to the window. It was light, being nothing more than a coarsely woven sack filled with straw. But it was thick and might just work with the mound of manure to cushion their fall, for he was certain now that they must jump.

He struggled to get it out the window, but when he did, he lined it up and let it drop on the mound of rotted manure.

"Quickly," he said to Erlissa.

She climbed up with his help until she squatted precariously on the windowsill.

"Hold on tight," he said. "Hang down by your arms first, so that your feet are as low as they can go before you let go."

She did as he said. He was glad that she was stronger than her lithe frame looked, for she held herself easily until she was positioned just right, and then with a gasp she dropped.

He watched her fall. It was a long way down, but she managed to land on her feet before slipping off the mattress and tumbling to the side.

For a moment he was worried, but she stood quickly and looked up at him.

He tossed down the staff, and she caught it deftly. Dogs began to bark, and the rooster crowed once more. It seemed louder now that the window was open, but was drowned out by a furious banging on the door. It was no longer just knocking, but an attempt to break it down.

Lanrik clambered up onto the sill. Both his feet were on it, and he had turned around so that he could hang down by his arms as Erlissa had, when the door crashed inward and timber from the splintered doorjamb flew into the room.

Brinhain stood framed in the doorway. He held his sword high. His face, just visible in the dim light, appeared twisted by emotion.

Lanrik had the sudden feeling that the captain was angry, not only because Erlissa had delayed his entry, but because he had conspired with the three robbers out of spite at what had happened during the afternoon, and that plan had failed. It made sense, for the robbers were too bold, and their chances of escape too slim with so many guards staying at the inn – unless they knew beforehand that any chase would be slow to start.

For a moment he stared straight into Brinhain's eyes. Hatred flashed in both directions. And, suddenly, there was something else too. Brinhain's expression altered. There was now recognition and understanding. He realized why Lanrik and Erlissa were trying to flee instead of seek help from the guards, as would have been normal. For a moment longer their gaze held, and then Lanrik dropped.

The ground sped up to meet him. Just like Erlissa, he landed on his feet, but then he slid and toppled sideways. Rolling, he stood up again and grabbed the mattress. Swiftly, he cast it aside so that the guards could not use it. Not that they needed to, for it would only take them moments to race down the stairs come around the yard to the back of the inn.

"Run!" he said. As always, Erlissa wasted no time asking questions. She knew he had a plan, and trusted him.

He raced to the stables and flung open the door. There were many stalls inside, one after another along a narrow corridor at their front. They made for the two closest stalls, opened them, and led the horses out. They were quiet animals, which was just as well. Lanrik knew his luck was good tonight, but it could not last much longer.

They were fine horses, and obviously belonged to the Royal Guard, for they were of a quality that ordinary citizens rarely rode except the nobility or those who raced in the Haranast.

They did not wait, but mounted them straight away. Lanrik led, easing his into a canter through the stable doorway. They were just in time. The guards were in the yard. He guided his mount around to face them, kicked it forward and charged them with a wild yell.

The guards scattered, leaping and diving, though one tried to grab his leg and pull him off. Lanrik looped his arms around the horse's neck and kicked out hard.

He got through, leaving the guards behind him, and glanced back to see that Erlissa was following close in his wake.

Once again they were riding barebacked, using nothing but headstalls and reins, but this would not be a long race. Either they lost any pursuit quickly, or they would likely be caught.

They came to the front of the inn. To their right was the bridge, and a path into the wild where his skill as a Raithlin would serve him well. To their left, the road led into the city, which he guessed the guards knew better than he did.

He did not hesitate. He kicked his horse into a gallop and Erlissa followed close behind. The hooves of the horses thudded loud along the empty road, and the cool dawn air rushed past.

It was still and peaceful all around them, but they raced with frantic purpose along the road. And they headed toward the city, for Lanrik was not willing to abandon his quest. With luck, they would have a momentary lead, for likely the guards, not used to riding bareback, would saddle their horses before they began their pursuit.

The road followed a long and gentle rise toward Gold Gate, the northern entry into Esgallien. To their left, the sun crested the horizon; a fiery ball that shot yellow-gold rays over the city. Towers glinted, stained-glass windows sparked to life and tiled roofs glowed with warm light. But the road remained gray beneath them as they bent low over the necks of their straining horses.

He could see the gate clearly now. It remained closed, but the soldiers who guarded it should open it at any moment. To either side ran the wall that encircled Esgallien.

Lanrik did not know if the gate would be open when they reached it. But if not, he had a plan. He always had a plan, although his inspiration had run to a low ebb in Erlissa's room with Brinhain hammering at the door. He did not like the feeling, and he hoped not to experience it again.

The wall loomed close. It was an ancient though solid structure, built of plastered brick. It rose thirty feet high and ten deep. It was less impressive than the one that surrounded Cardoroth, and the comparison brought home to him how fragile was the safety of the city that he loved.

The gate was still closed. He could see the soldiers who manned it milling around. Nearby, tall towers guarded either side of the entrance. Fifty-foot images of Conhain were carved in high relief on each one.

Esgallien's first king was clad in war raiment, helm and chain mail carefully depicted. In his hand he held a naked sword, ready to strike, the tip of each blade touching above the middle of the gate. It was a warning to enemy armies that breaching the walls would not be easy.

Sunlight lit the king's carved gaze, but his mighty feet were still in shadow. *Conhain!* Thought Lanrik. Dead a thousand years, yet still the beating heart of Esgallien society. In the nation of people that once he ruled, there must yet be those with the boldness to resist Ebona. She had conquered them by stealth rather than sword, but their courage would kindle one day, and then woe to her and Murhain.

They neared the gate. The soldiers opened it, but too late Lanrik and Erlissa slowed down. Their galloping was suspicious, and the men stood at the entry to the tunnel and barred their way.

Lanrik glanced back. Guards were on the road behind them. They had saddled their horses; a mistake they would regret, if only he and Erlissa could get inside the city.

He thought about trying to charge through, but in the narrow confines of the tunnel, where there was nowhere to go but forward, they would be at risk of sword strokes. He would not take that chance with Erlissa. Not unless talking his way through failed.

They pulled the horses up before the men.

One of the soldiers stepped forward. He was young, but Lanrik did not think he looked stupid. Even worse, he did not look gullible.

The man's hand was on the hilt of his sword.

"What's the hurry?"

"Why else would we hurry?" Lanrik said. "We're in need of haste." He glanced at Erlissa. "Tamril is a healer, and she's needed urgently in the city."

The soldier gazed at her carefully. All the while Lanrik knew their pursuers were galloping up the road behind them, but he resisted the urge to look. That would only serve to highlight his fear.

"You're in *so* much of a hurry that you're riding bareback?"

"Yes. It *is* that urgent." Lanrik thought quickly. He needed something more here, and he needed it fast.

"Her uncle is Faramond," he added.

"Faramond? As in the horse trainer?"

"How many other Faramonds do you know? Yes. It's *that* Faramond. The famous one. The one who trains the best horses to ever race in the Haranast." He leaned

37

forward and spoke earnestly. "Word reached her during the night that he collapsed. He needs her help. He's an old man, you know."

The soldier looked hesitant. Faramond was a beloved horse trainer. And few liked going to the Haranast to watch the races, and drink, better than young soldiers.

The man seemed inclined to let them through, but one of his companions raised an arm and pointed over their heads.

"It looks to me like they're being chased," the soldier said.

Everyone's eyes narrowed and looked back down the road. The Royal Guard were getting nearer, and they were not sparing their horses.

The young man looked at them hard. His hand was still on the sword hilt.

"Have you stolen these horses? Is that why you're riding bareback?"

"Look at them man!" Lanrik said heatedly. "They're quality horses. They're some of the finest you'll ever see. That should be proof enough that Tamril lives with her uncle, and that he needs her. Needs her now! And that's no pursuit. The Royal Guard don't chase horse thieves. They're our escort, but their horses aren't as fast as ours."

The soldier wavered.

Erlissa leaned forward. A single tear ran down her cheek, and her face took on an expression of frustration and fury.

"If my uncle dies, I'll tell the whole city that it was the guards at the gate who stopped me from getting to him in time. Let us through!"

The young man paled. It was a dangerous time in Esgallien. Trouble always made the races more popular as people sought a distraction. No one would want to be held responsible for the death of the most respected trainer in the last hundred years. But would that be enough? Lanrik could not tell, and in the distance the pursuit was catching up.

4. Hunted

Time slowed, and Lanrik felt the breath in his lungs catch and cease to flow. For a moment, their fates hung in the balance, and then, with a brisk wave to his men, the soldier moved to the side.

"Let them through," he said.

The men parted. Lanrik, resisting the urge to look behind, trotted through the gap and into the tunnel. Erlissa rode close beside him, and the clatter of hooves on the cobbled surface rang loud in the confined space. He thought he heard other noises too, perhaps yelling from those who pursued them, but it was too faint and dim to tell for sure.

After a few moments, they passed through the arch in the inner wall and rode beneath the shadow of Conhain's mighty towers. They were on the Hainer Lon, and inside the city, but that did not mean that the chase was over.

The great road ran ahead of them. It traveled far, all the way to River Gate, and crossed the heart of the city between. It was central to all Esgallien: thousands of stalls, shops, businesses and homes lined its sides, and long porticoes to left and right sheltered people from rain and sun alike. But the Hainer Lon offered little protection to fugitives.

Lanrik kicked his horse into a gallop, and Erlissa matched him. They raced ahead, for it was still quiet, but soon crowds would build and slow them to a walk. They would also be conspicuous, for hastening bareback as they were, they would draw everyone's gaze, and among the watches there would certainly be those quick to suspicion and even some ready to aid the Royal Guard.

What they needed now was stealth, rather than speed, and a place to hide and to disappear within the city, for they could not hope to evade a pursuit where the mass of people would slow them, remember them, and willingly or unwillingly, allow the Royal Guards to catch up.

Lanrik turned left down the first side street that offered what he needed. There was an inn, and though there were likely stables down the side or back of the yard, there were hitching posts at the front to tether horses.

He dismounted and led his horse toward a post.

"Look casual," he whispered.

There were several people nearby, and for all he knew there could also be Royal Guards in the inn. They must not draw attention to themselves, and yet they must act quickly.

They looped their reins through the holes in the post and started to walk off casually as though going about their normal business.

The further they went from their horses, the stranger it would look, but by the time someone noticed or thought to question them, it would be too late. However, before they were halfway down the street, they heard the sudden clatter of many hooves along the Hainer Lon. Lanrik glanced back over his shoulder.

Riders streamed past, but one abruptly halted.

"My horse!" the man shouted.

Lanrik and Erlissa ran. Looking casual would no longer serve them.

He took the lead, but Erlissa kept pace close behind him. Their pursuers jostled one by one into the street as they gave chase. For a moment, Lanrik heard them gather speed and close in, and then an intersection loomed and he took a right turn into an alleyway.

Ahead, the way was confined and buildings of ancient and crumbling brick rose steeply above them. They were tenement homes for some of the poorer citizens of Esgallien. This was a dangerous place, a haven for robbers and violent crime, and the sort of area that Lanrik would normally avoid, but the darkness and lack of room suited him at the moment.

They raced on. The alley was full of rubbish, and the cobbles beneath their feet were uneven and in ill repair. Water and muck gathered in potholes, and a foul smell hung heavy in the air.

Ignoring the signs of poverty and decrepitude, they raced ahead. Behind, struggling to ride two abreast, came the first of the guards. They were like two corks in one bottle, squeezing each other and stopping everything behind.

Lanrik saw another alley and darted left. This was wider, and there was a small market here. People milled around, talking or haggling over prices, and Lanrik took advantage of it.

"Royal Guards!" he shouted. "They're trying to kill everyone!"

Panic broke out. People had no trouble believing his words, a situation that might have surprised him had he not already met Brinhain and his men.

People, who only a moment before had been talking and laughing, now fled in a fever of fear. Some entered buildings and slammed doors shut, others raced along the street. At that moment, the first two guards turned the corner and their horses, covered in sweat, rushed into view.

The panic intensified, and Lanrik and Erlissa, right in the middle of a pack of running people, went with a smaller group that broke away and dived inside an open doorway.

It was a tenement building. There were already people inside, some crying, some screaming, but the last person to enter slammed the door and yelled for everyone to keep quiet. He put his ear to the timber and tried to hear what was happening outside.

Lanrik and Erlissa were already on the move. The horses could be heard through the door, though whether they had been seen entering the building or not, they could not tell. Nor did they wait to find out.

They went straight to a window at the back of the building, unbolted it, and clambered out into another alley.

It was dark here, even seedier than the last one if that was possible, but there were no horses and there were no people, either. They raced along it.

For the next few minutes they zigzagged through a half dozen more, running through those where nobody was present, and walking briskly in the others so as not to draw attention. They heard no horses, but they could hear intermittent yelling in the distance.

They were heaving for breath, and their legs trembled.

"We need to rest," Erlissa said.

She was right. They were nearly spent, and if they kept on going like this there was just as much chance of running into the guards by accident as escaping them. This part of the city was a maze, and they could turn into a narrow street at any moment and unwittingly come face to face with their pursuers.

On the other hand, the longer they delayed the more chance that troops would be called in to reinforce and widen the existing search.

They walked slowly now, carefully inspecting each street and only choosing crowded ones to walk down.

The city was becoming increasingly busy as the day grew older, and that was a help in hiding them.

They came to a wider street. A roofed colonnade ran to either side, and for a moment Lanrik though they were back on the Hainer Lon, but then he realized it was still too narrow for that. It was a market street of some sort though, and shops lined the way.

"We need a change of clothes," he said.

Erlissa nodded. "So much for our disguises. We'll have to alter our appearance completely again." She paused and looked around. "But I know this place. I've been here before, although it was a long time ago."

She took his hand and led him onto the portico off the street. They passed a stall that offered various savory breads for breakfast, and the sudden smell of food made him hungry, but they were still in danger and he ignored it.

Erlissa led him along a little further, and in moments they were in front of a small shop. The entrance was narrow, but inside many clothes hung from pegs in the wall or lay heaped in neat piles. It was exactly what they needed.

A black-haired woman with a bright smile approached.

"Can I help you?" she asked.

"Just looking," Erlissa answered noncommittally.

It was the beginning of a long session of haggling. Lanrik hated the custom, at least normally. He did not doubt that he often overpaid for the things that he bought, but he would rather that, and get what he wanted quickly, than play a game of words. But it served them well now, for a group of Royal Guards was riding slowly down the street. They looked carefully at everybody as they went, but though they tried, they could not see far inside the shops to either side.

He did not realize it for a moment, but the black-haired woman had come to stand close beside him.

"What's that noise?" she asked.

Lanrik only noticed it when she spoke, for it was in the distance. He tilted his head to hear better, and caught the sound of a long and winding note from a horn. No doubt the Royal Guard were calling for reinforcements. That might mean the City Watch as well as more of their own, but he was not going to tell her that.

"I'm not sure," he said.

Erlissa frowned. "Soldiers, I think. Probably the Royal Guard."

The woman hissed. "They're always looking for somebody these days." She looked as though she was about to say more, but then clamped her mouth shut.

Lanrik had the feeling that few people spoke freely in Esgallien anymore. It was dangerous, and to speak ill of the Royal Guard might be especially so.

The woman changed the subject. She was back to business now, as though the conversation had never started.

"Well, I think this one suits you." She held up a green dress, slim and elegant. It was perhaps one of the most expensive items in the shop, and he could see from Erlissa's expression that she liked it, although it was doubtful if the woman noticed the same subtle signs.

He relaxed. The haggling would continue a long time before the price of such a dress came down enough to do a deal, and they needed a rest.

Out in the street he saw more guards. This group was on foot, and he was worried that they would start a search of each shop. But it soon became apparent that they would not. They had no reason to believe that he and Erlissa were here, and they did not have enough men to search each street in this part of the city, house by house and shop by shop. Not yet, at any rate.

Erlissa finally settled on a price, and money changed hands. Lanrik, with his customary speed, picked out a green cloak. It would serve to hide his tunic.

As an afterthought, he also bought a wide-brimmed hat that caught his fancy. He was not used to wearing hats, preferring a Raithlin hood, but it would change his appearance nicely.

There were no guards in the street at the moment, and it was a good time to leave. He paid for his items swiftly, ignoring Erlissa's frown and the black-haired woman's faint smile, and they moved back out onto the portico.

"We need another alley," he said. "We have to change clothes as quickly as possible. We're still in the search area."

"I've seen several groups," she said.

"They're everywhere," he agreed.

They found an alley and moved down it.

Tenement houses rose up all around them, steep and dark and grim. It was filthy here, as it often was away from the main streets. Lanrik did not like it, as he did not like much of the city, and yet there was a kind of splendor and humanity to most of Esgallien that attracted him in a way that the wild lands that he loved could not.

Washing hung over low ropes, cheap and coarse clothes that seemed little improved by the cleaning process, and Lanrik put on his hat and cloak quickly. There was no one in the alley, but that did not mean that there were no eyes on them.

Erlissa changed too, even more quickly than he, and she hung her old garments up on the line.

They moved briskly away. At just that moment two Royal Guards turned into the alley. For a moment, Lanrik hesitated, but a moment only.

5. The Voice of Doom

There was no going back. That would only alert the guards and instigate a chase.

He casually put his arm around Erlissa. She felt like a tense deer about to spring.

"Keep going," he whispered calmly. "Pretend nothing is wrong."

They walked forward at a leisurely pace. The guards scrutinized them. Despite their cold-eyed gaze, they were young men; too young, Lanrik thought, to be Royal Guards. He wondered if Ebona had deliberately filled the organization with new recruits. She would not be the first to build a personal army of impressionable young men, and to indoctrinate them into unquestioning support for her goals and methods.

The guards said nothing, evidently fooled by the change of clothes and the pretense of a casual attitude.

Lanrik and Erlissa moved out of the alley and turned into a much wider thoroughfare.

"We were lucky," he said.

"I know," she replied with a shudder. "They gave me the creeps the way they looked at me. And that was without even recognizing us."

"There seem to be more and more of them all the time," Lanrik said.

"Do you think we should find somewhere to hide? Or should we try to get away from this part of the city altogether?"

Lanrik thought about it. "There are too many guards to stay here. They seem to be coming in from elsewhere, and I'm sure they'll have our descriptions. It can't just be because of what happened at the inn. They *know* I'm a Raithlin, and they'll keep on searching until they find me."

"Do you think they know who you are, apart from just being a Raithlin?"

"Brinhain might have recognized me as I dropped from the window. I'm sure he realized that I was a Raithlin – why else would the person who was attacked be the one to flee? But it was more than that. I think he figured out a bunch of things in that last moment, our identities among them. If so, Ebona will spare no effort to catch us. We can't hide here. Each hour might bring more men, and eventually they'll search every building. I think we'd be better off taking our chances on the street and getting as far away as we can."

They walked ahead. Lanrik did not try to conceal his face with the broad-brimmed hat. That would only make it obvious that he was trying to hide. Instead, he walked with his head high. Better to be seen, and not recognized, than to be less easily seen but looked at more closely.

The morning passed, and the city filled with ever-larger crowds. There were guards too, standing on corners, walking down streets, mounted and on foot. The City Watch was everywhere too, but they seemed less keen on the search.

After a while the racket of blowing horns died down. They sighted the guards less often, and then suddenly there were none at all. They had finally broken free of the net that sought to contain them, and they abandoned pretense of leisurely walking for a brisk pace as they strode through the thick crowds.

"Do you know where we are?" Lanrik asked.

"I've got a fair idea. I don't know this part of the city well, but I've been here several times before. The Hainer Lon should be a few streets to our right." She paused a moment. "But the real question is this – where do you want to go?"

Lanrik did not hesitate. "The Merenloth. We need to see Bragga Mor. And the sooner the better. It should be a good place to hide too. It's always crowded there."

"Should we risk the Hainer Lon, or stay on the back streets?"

"The Hainer Lon would be quicker, but I've got a feeling that plenty of Royal Guards will be traveling down it to reinforce the search for us. Better to avoid them because there's no way to know if they've already got our description."

They kept to the side streets as the morning wore on. They were tired, not only physically but also mentally, for fear was just as exhausting as running.

After a while, Lanrik recognized where they were.

"The Merenloth is close," he said.

He led the way and slipped up a side street. Almost immediately the crowd swelled, and the noise of many people talking, the din of traders selling wares and children playing grew loud. They stepped onto the Hainer Lon and pressed ahead.

The great road of Esgallien seethed with people. It was a good place in its own way to hide, at least while they were on foot and there was no immediate pursuit. Walking along it reminded him of how large the city was. Tens of thousands of people dwelt here, and if they were somber at the inn, they were less so here. And yet he still caught an undercurrent of fear that he had never seen before. Some of the shops were closed and boarded up. Fire had reduced others to dilapidated shells, and private guards stood watch in front of the homes and shops of the wealthy.

At that moment, Lanrik stopped dead in his tracks. To the right, a once-grand building smoldered. Smoke curled up from the ends of several long beams of blackened timber, and the smell of wet ash made the air acrid. What once was a two-story house, with elaborate balconies and a plastered portico, was now a ruin of cracked bricks and collapsed roof tiles.

"What is it?" Erlissa asked.

"It's burnt down," Lanrik said softly.

"I've seen several others like that," she replied.

"Yes, I saw them too. But this was a Raithlin home. I knew the five men who lived here. They rented the house from a nobleman."

"Do you think Ebona did it?"

"Who else? She hates us."

Erlissa frowned. "I know that she hates the two of us. We've given her plenty of reasons. By why does she hate the Raithlin so much?"

"We have skills. Skills that can be used against her." He thought about it a bit more. "Also, I suspect that it's because we stand for everything that she hates. We're an old organization. We date back to Conhain himself, and if the stories are true we were devoted to him. She wouldn't have liked us then, and she sees us now as a rally point for the people, for we represent the things that Esgallien admires the most. She would want to ensure that no Raithlin lived who could rouse the people to fight her."

They moved on, their mood somber now, until they passed the middle of the city. The ground sloped upward slightly, and they soon came to the Merenloth. It stood on the left side of the Hainer Lon. Massive columns of carved granite flanked its entrance. Beyond, were hundreds of curved rows of stone benches terraced into the slope overlooking the stage. Thousands of people could sit here, and see and hear every movement and word of the performers.

A large crowd gathered inside now. The Merenloth was not full, but nearly so. Behind the stage the large surface of a many-storied building threw back the voice of the current speaker onto the crowd. Even as Lanrik and Erlissa stood at the entrance, they caught the words of an ancient lay telling of the Halathrin and their struggles against elugs and other enemies in the years predating the founding of Esgallien.

Lanrik did not know the performer. It was not Bragga Mor, nor could he be seen anywhere, but there were dozens of men seated on special benches near the stage, several of them wearing the distinctive many-colored cloak of the bards, and he could easily be among that group.

Lanrik and Erlissa passed inside. It was warm here, the heat from many people filling the amphitheater, and yet it was eerily quiet, for Esgalliens considered it rude to speak when a performer was on the stage.

The bard finished, and his words echoed back into the crowd from the brickwork behind him. It remained quiet for a moment longer, and then a loud applause rose and swelled strangely in the Merenloth.

The clapping died down, and then another man took the stage. He wore the simple white robes and customary oak-leaf brooch that Esgallien's philosophers favored.

Lanrik held Erlissa's hand. The crowd was thick as they worked their way down a long aisle between rows of stone benches. They could get no closer than the top level of seats, high above the stage.

The philosopher was a good way below them, and yet they saw and heard him clearly. He had started to speak.

His voice was soft, but buoyed and magnified by the Merenloth, it rang with quiet surety.

"People of Esgallien," he said. "These are troubled times. And in such days, there are few who give better counsel than the wise old men and women who have seen turmoil before and passed into calm again. These oldsters know how the bad days begin. And how they end." He paused. "I speak to you now not as a philosopher, but as a messenger, for I have spent much time listening to our grandfathers and grandmothers, and I will report their words to you now."

The man spoke fluently. Everyone listened, and a deep hush fell over the crowd. Yet in that moment of perfect quiet, Lanrik saw something that he did not like. There were Royal Guards near the stage. He did not think they were looking for him. They were seated, stony faced and straight backed, on their benches. He realized that there must be twenty of them, and their expressions worried him. They looked void of emotion, their eyes staring and their mouths clamped into tight lines.

The speaker paid them no heed. "The oldsters tell me that there are beautiful women. Smart women. Kindhearted women. And, for myself, I do not doubt that most husbands here know their wives are all three."

This brought a chuckle from the crowd, but when the philosopher continued, his voice carried a new note.

"The oldsters also tell me that there is yet one more type. The beautiful one. The one with skin that glows and eyes that shine and a voice that makes a man want to sing. But for all her beauty, there is darkness in her heart. It is a cold thing, heavy with malice. It beats to the rhythm of wickedness. Trouble, suffering and woe are its lifeblood."

The crowd stirred, but remained deathly silent. They knew of whom he spoke, and so too did the Royal Guards. One by one, they stood.

The speaker did not look at them. "We have one such among us. Her name is Ebona. And she is as wicked as she is beautiful."

"Enough!" yelled one of the guards.

The philosopher turned to him.

"Can the truth no longer be voiced in Esgallien?"

The guard drew his sword. "See this blade? It's the only truth that I know. And its word is final."

"Will you kill me then, just for speaking?"

The crowd, quiet until then, began to stir. There was anger in their sudden shouts.

One voice rose above them all, though Lanrik could not see him.

"Let him speak!" the voice said. Others took up the call, until it became a chant and the Merenloth thrummed with it.

Let him speak! Let him speak. Let him speak!

The guard looked around, doubt and surprise on his face. He spoke quickly to his comrades, and then they all drew their blades.

The guard, resolved now to act, stepped toward the philosopher, and the other guards faced the crowd.

The philosopher stood still. Whether in fear, disbelief, or defiance, Lanrik could not tell. Too late he moved, trying to step back as the guard darted toward him. The long sword ran him through in one quick motion.

The guard withdrew the blade, and when he did so the philosopher reeled away, blood staining his white robes, while red drops dripped from the still-raised blade.

The philosopher fell to his knees. His hands clamped tight against the wound. He did not utter a sound, and remained that way for several seconds. Then the life went from him. He dropped to the ground and lay still.

The crowd, for a moment shocked and silent, suddenly began to scream. Some made for the exit; some edged closer to the guards. But the guards began to swing their swords in a defensive motion, and moved forward themselves.

The crowd backed off. Everything was in a state of flux, and then the momentum shifted. Now, the crowd just wanted to get out of the Merenloth.

Lanrik watched in horror. He had never seen anything like it before, nor even heard of it. The Merenloth had always been a place where people freely spoke their beliefs. Arguments were common, but violence, especially a killing, was unthinkable. He knew things were bad under the influence of Ebona, but to see something so callous with his own eyes was shocking.

He broke out of his stupor and took hold of Erlissa's arm.

"Let's go!" he said.

She did not need any convincing. Nor was there much choice. The crowd was moving. It flowed like a great river and rushed out between the pillars at the exit like a fountain. They were swept up within it.

Erlissa nudged him. "There!" she said. She pointed to a tall figure ahead in the crowd.

Lanrik did not know what she meant at first, but then he saw what she had seen. Bragga Mor was ahead of them. His face was red, and his expression thunderous. He was clearly in a rage at the turn of events, and yet even he, influential as he was, dared not stay. He must flee with the rest of the crowd.

Lanrik held Erlissa's hand. The crowd was wild and pressing in all around them. They could not afford to become separated from each other.

He worked his way as best he could among the bumping and jostling people toward Bragga Mor. It might be their only chance to ever speak with him.

The panic of the crowd had not lessened. Several times people fell and screamed. And yet, things had not quite tipped into madness. He saw no one trampled, but many helping hands reach out to assist the fallen to their feet. Yet in the push and shove of things he made little headway, and Bragga Mor's many-colored cloak disappeared from view near the exit.

They soon passed between the granite columns themselves. There were people everywhere, but at least there was increasingly room to move. Many people ran, though most just hastened away with a look of shock on their faces and their heads bowed.

"There!" Erlissa said again. She had seen Bragga Mor once more. They ran themselves. It did not look suspicious now in the panic all around them, and they caught up swiftly to the bard, for he did not run. He strode ahead, as though he had a definite destination in mind, and not as though he was fearful.

Lanrik studied him for a moment. It was rumored that the man was a great swordsman, though he carried no blade now. At least, none that was visible. Yet a short sword might well be concealed beneath the cloak.

After a moment, Lanrik leveled with him.

"Bragga Mor. I need to speak with you."

The bard glanced at him, but did not slow his stride.

"Get home, boy. Get home while you can, and stay there."

Lanrik held his gaze. "I am home. *This*," he swung his arm in a wide arc, "is my home. And I would protect it."

That got the bard's attention. He stopped still and looked hard at him for a moment. His glance flickered to

Erlissa, and he gave her a slight bow, before looking back at Lanrik.

"Listen, boy. The streets aren't safe today. They may never be safe again. Get home, and take your lady friend with you. For the last few months Esgallien has been full of heroes like you. Most of them are now lying dead in dark pits. Don't become one of them."

Bragga Mor gave them both a stern look and strode ahead again.

Lanrik hesitated. This was not going as he would like, and he had to make a fast decision if he was to retrieve the situation. There was risk to what he must now do, and yet it had to be done. He thought he was a good judge of character, but if he was wrong, he might just as well knock on the Witch-queen's own door and hand himself in.

"I'm a friend of the Lindrath," he said quietly.

Bragga Mor stopped as though his legs had turned to stone. For a moment, he did not turn around. He stood there, looking like one of the statues in Conhain Court, while he made decisions of his own.

Lanrik waited, and said no more.

After a moment, the bard turned. "Listen, boy. I don't have time for this. And you should know better, young though you are. What you just said could get us both killed. And for what? Anybody could say that he was a friend to the Lindrath."

What the bard said was true. Bragga Mor stared at him. His freckled face was still red. His gingery beard bristled, and his curly hair looked like fire. He was an angry man, and in a moment he would turn and walk away.

"I'm not a boy," Lanrik said. "And though anyone could claim to be a friend of the Lindrath, not everybody carries a token to prove it."

Bragga Mor's eyes fixed on him like an eagle watching its prey. But Lanrik waited. He glanced to the side while a group of people hurried past them.

When there was no one near enough to see, he placed a hand on the hilt of his sword and drew the blade a few inches from its sheath.

Bragga Mor watched him. For a moment his face was blank, and then Lanrik saw recognition in his eyes as he noticed the trotting fox motif etched into the blade. The bard's eyes widened.

Lanrik slammed back the blade. "I'm not a boy. I'm exactly who I say I am, and I need to talk to you."

The face of Bragga Mor was blank again. He was unreadable. He showed no anger, or fear, or frustration. Nor was there any indication of loyalty or surprise. The bard was adept at hiding his thoughts, and if it was on his mind to betray them in order to gain favor with the Witch-queen, Lanrik could not tell. But he knew this: the Lindrath had called the man a friend.

"We can't talk here," Bragga Mor said finally.

The bard walked ahead once more, striding out with his long legs, and they walked with him. But he did not take them far. Nor did he speak again while they remained on the Hainer Lon, and there was a chance of being overheard.

After a few minutes, he turned abruptly and walked beneath an elaborate portico. It was dark under the shade of the tiled roof, and a wide shop entrance, flanked by marble statues opened before them.

Lanrik could not see inside, but a young woman stood at the entrance, and she smiled at the bard.

"Your usual seat, Sir?"

"No. I'll need a table for three today."

The girl curtsied and led them through the doorway.

Lanrik was distrustful. He did not know Bragga Mor, still less this place, and there was likely only one exit if it was a trap. Still, he took a deep breath and followed the bard.

Erlissa took his hand and squeezed it. It was her way of saying that she understood the risk they were taking, and that she agreed with his judgment.

They entered a dark room. Thick rugs lay on the floor, and scented candles burned in ornate holders. There were only a few people here, but they all had the look of wealth about them. Lanrik felt out of place in his ordinary clothes, and he removed his hat.

The girl led them to a booth at the back of the room. It was quiet, with no tables nearby, and they would be able to speak in privacy.

"Tea," the bard said to the girl. "And for my guests also."

She curtsied and walked away.

Lanrik guided Erlissa to one of the cushioned seats, and then sat himself. He made sure that he faced the entrance.

Bragga more noticed and smiled for the first time.

"You haven't decided to trust me yet?"

"No. But I need information, and I think you have it. If this is a trap, I can see the entrance. More importantly, I'm close to you."

Bragga Mor took no offense at the implied threat.

"Yes, that's fair enough. But think on this. You're just as likely to be a trap for me as the other way around."

The girl returned, and they did not speak for a moment. She deftly served them three mugs of hot tea, a concoction that Lanrik had never drunk before, but one that the aristocracy favored. He tasted it. It was not unlike herbal drinks that he had sometimes made in the wild on cold nights, except that it was sweetened with honey.

Before the girl left she gave Bragga Mor a white cloth and a bowl of water. Lanrik wondered what it was for. He understood when the bard wetted the cloth and started to dab at droplets of blood that stained his shirt. He must have been close to the killing in the Merenloth.

Bragga Mor noticed his glance. "I told the philosopher not to speak. He should've listened."

For the first time, Lanrik caught a glimpse of the man behind the public mask. He was furious, and for just cause. The killing of the philosopher was a shocking deed, but it would be more so to one who knew him, as Bragga Mor likely did.

"We don't have much time," the bard said. "I'll not stay here long, and after that I doubt we'll see each other again. So ask what you want, and I'll give what answers I can."

Lanrik got straight to the point. "Do you know what happened to the Raithlin?"

Bragga Mor sighed. "The king never liked your lot. It seems that the Witch-queen likes you even less, though. Anyway, some of them spoke against her when Murhain invited her into the city. That was a mistake. She wasted no time in having them killed. And soon after others, even those who hadn't spoken, were taken from their homes. They disappeared, and haven't been seen since. Not that you have to be a Raithlin for that to happen. Many others have disappeared too."

He looked around him casually, making sure that no one was near, before he continued.

"The Raithlin went into hiding after that, but they still spoke out. They spread dissent through the city, and it must have lit a fire under Ebona. She didn't like it at all. But somehow, slowly and surely, she rooted them out from their hiding places. They were taken, and no doubt killed. For a while, barely a week went by without a house being torched or some rumor surfacing of another fight. And fights there were, for none of them went willingly."

Bragga Mor did not drink his tea. His eyes were downcast, and he spoke softly, fluently and with a rich voice that drew a vivid picture for them.

"I saw one of the killings myself," he said. "It was near the palace. I knew him. His name was Gilhain, and he leaped out of the crowd to try to kill the Witch-queen. Knives flew from his hands as he ran, but they had no effect. They struck her, but bounced away as though they had been thrown into a brick wall. He drew his sword then, but before he reached her she flung fire at him from outstretched arms. Otherworldly it was. I've never seen the like. It burned and sizzled through the air and knocked him down."

Bragga Mor paused. Lanrik and Erlissa exchanged a glance. He read in her eyes that she recognized the Raithlin's name. Gilhain had welcomed them back from Galenthern when they crossed the ford to bring word of the elug army approaching Esgallien. It seemed a long time ago now.

The bard took a sip of tea. His hands trembled slightly, but his voice was steady.

"Gilhain somehow got back on his feet. He was burning all over, but he ran at her. The steel of his blade flared white hot. She flung flame at him once more. He tottered, but only fell when Royal Guards filled him with arrows. He died cursing her name, and I shall never forget it, for I saw bravery then that a thousand lays of the old days never showed me."

He took another sip of tea, and Erlissa put a hand over Lanrik's on the table.

"The Raithlin disappeared from Esgallien after that, however many were left by that stage. Perhaps half of them."

"Where did they go?" Lanrik asked.

"No one knows. Not for sure. But the word is that they went to Galenthern. They can live there, and the Witch-queen cannot hunt them. Or if she can, it would take her a long time."

Lanrik had a feeling that this was true. The plains were vast, and the swamps impenetrable. It would take decades to track them down there, and it would not be worth the effort. Even an army would struggle to do the job.

He had one more question. He struggled to ask it, for he feared the answer. But Bragga Mor surprised him with one of his own.

"Any Raithlin in the city would know as much as what I just told you. Or more. So you haven't been here."

The bard looked at him hard. "You're Lanrik, aren't you?" He shifted his gaze. "And you, my dear, must be Erlissa."

There was little point in lying. "Yes," Lanrik said.

Bragga Mor nodded slowly. "I saw you fight in the sword tournament of the Spring Games, but that was quite a while ago, and I couldn't be sure it was you. You and Mecklar were in the final. For what it's worth, I think you should've won."

Lanrik shrugged. "Maybe. But as you say, that was a while ago. All that really matters is that I won the next time – when it counted most."

Bragga Mor gave him an appraising look.

"Small wonder that no one has seen Mecklar for a long time. You know, he used to drink in this very shop.

I said hello to him many a time. I never drank with him, though."

Lanrik gathered his courage and forced himself to ask one more question.

"What happened to the Lindrath?"

Bragga Mor let out a long breath and slowly shook his head. When he spoke, his words were like the voice of doom.

"Of him, I know more than the other Raithlin. He did not escape the city."

"Is he dead?" Lanrik asked.

Bragga Mor looked away. But before he did, there was pity in his eyes.

6. A Twitch of Flame

The hair on the back of Brinhain's neck prickled.

He would *not* show fear in front of his men. They were scared too, but that was of no consequence. All that mattered was that they thought he, as their leader, was unperturbed. It did not matter if it was a lie.

He stood straight and tall. The great door to Esgallien's throne room opened. The massive oak panel, heavy enough that five men could not lift it, swung easily on its gold-plated hinges at the touch of one of the soldiers stationed there. They were Royal Guards, as he would expect in the palace. It worried him that he did not recognize them, though.

The door came to a stop. He walked past the guards slowly, eying each of them for a moment, but they showed not even the barest flicker of respect or acknowledgement of his rank. He was a captain, and they were glorified butlers with swords. It was one more thing to worry about. If he failed Ebona, there were others to take his place – a seemingly unending string of them.

He promised himself that he would not fail her.

His boots, and those of several of his most trusted men, echoed hollowly in the vast chamber as they crossed the polished timber floor. He took one look at Ebona, and wished that he had brought his whole company. Yet he wondered if even an army would protect him should she want him dead.

The queen sat on her throne. Her gaze, cold and remote, drove into him like a spear. She showed no obvious anger, though a faint flush of red colored her face. He sensed that she restrained herself, and his heart skipped a beat.

King Murhain sat on a throne next to her. He had no wife, for he and Ebona were not married. In truth, she had no right or claim to rule, and yet she invoked a sense of authority that he did not. A fool he looked, staring vacant eyed at the woman who had seduced him, waiting for her to speak in order that he might know how to proceed.

Brinhain bowed. When he looked up, he caught his breath. Ebona was standing. She wore no royal robes, or crown, nor any jewels. She was clad in a simple linen dress, white and clean, cinched by a red belt. And yet she looked regal. Her figure was slim and tall. Nobility shone from her face. Her cheekbones were high, and the gaze of her wide-set eyes was clear and bright. The long tumble of her blonde hair surpassed any crown.

Brinhain understood how the king had fallen. He felt himself yearn for her favor, but she looked at him with a hard gaze.

"We have received your messages," Ebona said. She glanced at the king, and he smiled at her. "And they disappoint us."

She stepped closer. He noticed for the first time that her feet were bare, and yet she seemed to tower above him.

"Strange, that when tidings are good you come yourself, but only send messengers to report bad news, unless summoned. Perhaps you're scared of me?"

Brinhain knew that nothing but the truth would do.

"Yes, My Queen. I'm scared of you."

Ebona pursed her lips. "Then you are not a *complete* fool."

She stepped closer. Her feet made no noise on the timber floor.

"And yet, you have still failed me. Not only did you allow a Raithlin to escape your grasp, but the one above all others that I want most. Not to mention the wretched *witch-girl* that accompanies him."

Brinhain did not like the tone that had crept into her voice. He knew that she hated Lanrik and Erlissa, but until that moment he had underestimated how much. Abhorrence throbbed in her every word.

"I'm sorry, My Queen."

Ebona placed a hand on his shoulder, and he felt goose bumps rise all over his skin.

"Are you? Or do you mean that you *will* be?"

Brinhain's heart thudded. "I won't fail you again, My Queen. Even as we speak, hundreds of men search the city. I won't stop until I bring your enemies to you."

Ebona shook her head slowly. "You are quick to move onto other matters. But we are yet to establish what your punishment will be."

Sweat beaded his face. His sensed his men shuffle back. He wanted to do the same, but dared not.

"What punishment could be worse than failing you, My Queen? Except not being able to redeem myself."

"What punishment, indeed?" she said.

She stepped close and draped an arm around him. Lightly, like a wisp of air, she moved behind him. He felt her hot breath on his neck. But when she spoke, it was to Murhain.

"O King!" she said. "Ruler of men. Head of the mighty nation of Esgallien. Come! Tell me what you think. Speak to me from the wellspring of your wisdom. What punishment is fitting for the captain's failure?"

Murhain frowned, as though deep in thought. His gaze wavered between Ebona and the floor.

"He failed you, My Queen."

"Yes," said Ebona. There was a hint of impatience in her voice. "But his punishment?"

Brinhain did not think the king was capable of deciding what he wanted for breakfast, let alone anything else. Was Ebona poisoning him? There were drugs that took a man's mind before they stole his life.

Murhain focused on the floor as though he could read the secrets to life there.

"Kill him," he said at length.

Brinhain felt Ebona behind him. One of her arms was draped over his shoulder. Her hand, with its strange toe-like thumb, rested on his chest. She must feel the beating of his heart, sense the panic rising through his body.

"Well," she said. "Death you have earned. And a slow one, too." She paused. Her fingers tapped his chest to the rhythm of his heartbeat. "You know, don't you, that I could make you die, and rouse you, only to make you die again? It's a game I could play all night."

Brinhain tried to speak. His voice faltered in his throat.

"What was that, dear? Did you say you want to play that game?"

"No! My Queen." He gasped the words out. He felt ashamed to be unmanned in front of his men. Worse, to show weakness to her. His glance fell on the king, and a thought occurred to him. Better to die a man, than live as a fool.

"I failed you, Ebona. It was a mistake. Kill me if you choose, but do not think you have a more loyal servant. Or a more capable one."

He felt her stiffen behind him. Her hand on his chest froze in place. His heart raced wildly, but he no longer cared.

She laughed. It was the light sound of a carefree young girl, though she was anything but.

"Oh! That was well done. Perhaps you have some virtues after all."

He remained silent. The king seemed to have lost interest in proceedings. His gaze roved aimlessly over the room's exquisite murals, tapestries and statuettes, before wandering back to Ebona. There they rested a while, as though finding peace in his adulation of her.

"We shall spare him now, shall we not, O King?"

"Yes," Murhain answered. "Spare him. He is a true and valiant servant."

Ebona moved once more. She uncoiled herself from him. One moment he felt her behind him, and the next she stood in front. Her eyes gazed into his, blue-green wells that sparked with thoughts and emotions that he could not fathom, but wanted to know. He understood how easy it would be to fall under her sway. He blinked, and pressed the tip of his boot into the floor. The pain from his gout-afflicted toe flared to life.

She grinned at him suddenly. "Perhaps you can serve me yet. At least, for a little while longer."

Her bright eyes shifted to the guards that he had brought.

"Which one of your men has served you best?"

Brinhain did not hesitate. "Caracas, My Queen."

"Come forward, Caracas," she ordered.

Slow footsteps sounded behind him. It was the reluctant tread a man who wanted to go nowhere fast. Brinhain did not blame him, but things had taken a new turn. There would be no punishment now.

Caracas drew level.

The queen looked him over. "You know, Caracas, that I have powers?"

"Yes, My Lady."

"And I have used them. Yes, I have tried to locate Lanrik and Erlissa, but something wards them from my sight."

Brinhain saw her eyes change. There was suppressed anger there. She did not like to be stymied. It infuriated her, though she kept a tight control of herself.

"That means," she continued, "that I must find them another way. The lòhren Aranloth protects them. He thinks he is smart, but I am smarter. I, who walked this world long ages before he was born. I, to whom all people will one day bow. Even the lòhren, before I kill him. And I have a plan. These fools think they can come to my city, and do as they please. Well, let them! I know what they want. First and foremost, Lanrik will seek news of his brother Raithlin. More than that, he will try to discover what happened to the Lindrath. They say he loves him like a father. Well, we shall put that to the test. The whole city knows where I left him. Lanrik will soon learn, and it is there that we shall catch him."

"I'll set a watch and arrest him," Brinhain promised.

"You said that last time, when he traveled down the Carist Nien toward the Angle." She looked at him hard, and he shivered. "I'll not make the mistake of relying on you again. This time, I'll give you help."

She turned to Caracas. "Step closer."

Caracas obeyed, yet Brinhain sensed his reluctance. So too did Ebona.

"Come, there is nothing to be afraid of. This will be to your benefit. You'll see, and thank me in the end. After all, what man does not wish to be stronger, faster and a better fighter? What man would turn away from the chance to be near invincible? I shall give you powers to overcome Lanrik, and the witch-girl with him. Would you like that?"

"Yes, My Queen," Caracas answered slowly.

"Good. I see that your desire to serve me burns white-hot. And so I shall permit you to do so."

She stepped lightly toward him. Brinhain had a bad feeling, and yet whatever was going to be done would not affect him. He watched, transfixed by curiosity, part-jealous of the sorcerous gift Ebona would bestow on the man, but part-expecting that it would come at a price.

Ebona's feet glided soundlessly over the timber flooring. Distantly, he heard the king hum to himself, but he paid Murhain no heed. King he might be, but in Esgallien's court, the Witch-queen alone dispensed reward or punishment.

She came to a halt. Her head tilted a little as she considered Caracas. One moment she stood like that, poised and still, and the next her arm shot forth as though released from a bow. Her hand did not pierce flesh, but it gripped and squeezed. Her fingers, like iron pincers, caught and crushed his throat.

Caracas was strong, but it seemed that he was no match for the queen. He struggled, trying to break free. He dropped down, twisted to the side and reeled back. But whatever he did, he only managed to move a little. His face reddened, and desperation etched his features. He started to strike at her arms, but she shrugged the blows off. He tried to hit her face, but she shook him as a child shakes a doll, and he flailed uselessly.

His death came swiftly. One moment he was thrashing wildly, but soon after his movements were feeble. When he slumped in her grip, she let him collapse to the floor.

Caracas's body was limp. He looked up from bulging eyes, but there was no flicker of life within them. The skin of his neck was red, but where Ebona's iron-like grip had fixed to it, white marks outlined her fingers and thumb.

Brinhain gulped. He looked at the Witch-queen, and gulped again.

Ebona circled the corpse. Her feet moved lightly, as though she danced, and fire sprang from the floor wherever she stepped. There was no smoke.

Through the twisting flames, Brinhain saw the timber beneath. The wood remained undamaged. This was sorcery of a kind that he had not seen before, and he tried to gulp again but his mouth was dry. He made a gurgling sound. Ebona ignored him.

The flames leapt higher. She moved away from them and stood next to him. He felt the heat of the fire, or of her body; he could no longer tell which was which. She lifted her hands above her head, and the flames rose higher at her command. The light was blinding, and yet the warmth in the throne room lessened. It swiftly grew cold.

Brinhain looked around. The king sat idly, whispering to himself and oblivious to the powers that Ebona unleashed, and yet in the corners of the room there were shadows. There should not be, for the light of Ebona's flame was bright. But shadows there were, and they danced closer.

Brinhain did not move. The witch stood still beside him, and whatever was happening in the room, he knew the safest place was next to her.

The shadows flowed. They leaped and capered to their own rhythm. They neared the bright flames, merged with them, and writhed now as one, twirling, twitching and climbing into the smokeless air.

A moment they flared with blinding light, and then they subsided. Or, he thought, they moved inward. They flickered over the corpse, touching it, caressing it, smothering it.

The right hand of Caracas began to jerk. His left followed soon after. And then his whole body shuddered. The corpse came to its knees, and then swayed to its feet. It was a thing of dead flesh, and yet it twitched with the flame of life.

Caracas raised his arms. Fire leaped to his face, and then ran all over his body. His mouth opened. He screamed, but there was no sound, only a stream of shadow-fire.

The sorcerous flame burned skin, peeled patches away to expose red flesh. Eyebrows withered and the hair on his head ignited like a torch. His clothes, half burned away, half melted onto his body, smoked and crackled.

Caracas, or that which was Caracas, writhed in agony, but slowly the fire subsided. It did not go out, rather it seeped inside him. His eyes flickered with it. Smoke curled from his wide-flared nostrils. He stood almost still now. His face was recognizable, but he stared blankly ahead.

The fire disappeared, but his charred body still twitched as though it danced inside him. His hands flicked without cessation. His shoulders shrugged and jerked with a life of their own.

Brinhain retched. He tasted bile in the back of his mouth. When the nausea passed, he looked up to see Ebona watching him.

"Go," she said. "Caracas will obey you, but once he finds Lanrik and the girl, nothing will control him. He must kill them, pass the flame onto them, or he will never be rid of it, himself."

She turned and walked toward her throne. "Go," she said over her shoulder, "and do not return until it's with the tidings that I most wish to hear. And if you don't bring them, then you will suffer. Go!"

Brinhain bowed to Ebona's back. He turned swiftly and strode away. His men did not look at him. He smelled their fear, even above his own. The corpse of Caracas twitched and lurched behind him.

He left the throne room and breathed the air beyond as though it was the sweetest thing in the world. The pain in his big toe slowed him, but not much. He was filled with determination. He would not fail Ebona again. *He would not.* Lanrik and Erlissa were as good as dead, and if Ebona was right, he knew just where to wait for them.

7. A Message in Blood

Bragga Mor spoke, and Lanrik listened carefully.

"They captured the Lindrath," the bard said simply. "The details aren't important. All that matters is that he didn't leave the city with the Raithlin – he chose to stay and help the forces opposing the Witch-queen. What was left of them, anyway."

"Then there's still resistance to her?" Lanrik asked. He was trying to give himself time to brace for the worse news that would follow.

"Well, in truth, the whole city opposes her, but the people have learned not to voice their opinions. And especially not to act on them. It's certain death. All rebellion has ceased. What I meant is that he tried to keep it alive, even after it died."

Lanrik was not so sure about that. The people might accept their situation now, but that did not mean they had given up hope of changing it. They were like any conquered people in history: when the time came, they would rise up against their oppressor.

Bragga Mor continued. "There were rumors, of course. The city is always full of rumors. I heard from several sources, usually reliable ones, that he escaped. Unfortunately, it was wishful thinking. Or lies."

"He's a prisoner then?"

The bard shook his head. He looked grim. "No. Two days ago, the Witch-queen killed him."

They were simple words, and Lanrik had prepared himself to hear them, yet they still shook him. He had trouble thinking clearly. For a moment, memories flooded his mind. He had spent so much time with the Lindrath. They were good times, too. Training, walking across Galenthern, practicing sword skills, but most of all just talking. Lanrik absorbed his words, always eager to hear any stories, and there were plenty of them. He modelled himself on the older man's behavior, for he was not just the leader of the Raithlin, but a kind and generous man, swift to help a new recruit, slow to rebuke them. He was everything that Lanrik ever wanted to be. It was hard to believe that he would never hear his voice, or see his sudden smile again.

"Are you sure?" he said to the bard after a while. "Maybe that's just another rumor."

Bragga Mor looked at him through tired eyes. "The Witch-queen herself verified it." He hesitated, and then went on. "She wanted the city to know that he was dead. She made it known that he was tortured, and that she had learned from him the names of those who opposed her before he was executed. As proof of her words, she chained his body to the palace gate. It would be a lesson, she proclaimed, of what it means to disobey her."

It was a callous deed, and Lanrik grew angry at the savagery of it.

"Has no one taken the body down?"

"The queen forbade it. There are Royal Guards nearby, and she promised that anybody who tried to remove him would die a similar death. He must hang there, she decreed, until nothing is left but bones and the memory of what happens to those who oppose her."

Lanrik rested his head in his hands, and Erlissa put an arm around him. The bard fell silent and watched, for there was nothing more to say.

It was the worst possible news to Lanrik, even if he was expecting it. He tried to block his feelings. They would do neither he nor the Lindrath any good now.

Instead, he concentrated on what must be done to help the city. He had to learn more about Ebona, and the Royal Guards. For instance, why did she feel the need to make such an obvious example of the Lindrath? Was it because some still opposed her? If so, it would be his job to find them. Who were they? Where were they? And likewise, how many Royal Guards were there, and would they all fight for her?

His mind raced with ideas, but grief could not be denied, and it washed over him in ever-bigger waves. He could not hold it at bay. He lowered his head to the table and squeezed his eyes shut.

"That's an end to it," Bragga Mor said gently to Erlissa. "The Lindrath was a good friend to me, and I don't doubt that one day we'll be free of the Witch-queen, but that time is long away."

"Don't be so sure," Erlissa answered. "There are those who oppose her, the lòhrens among them."

Bragga Mor grunted. "They've offered no help so far."

"Have they not? Why do you think *we're* here?"

The bard was silent for a moment as he considered that.

"Well, perhaps hope is higher than I thought. But it'll take more than a Raithlin and a young girl to save the city."

"True, and yet it's a start. Also, this girl has faced Ebona before. And survived. Keep in mind as well that she was beaten in Conhain's time. She learned fear then, and we'll teach it to her again."

Bragga Mor looked her over. At length, he grinned.

"Well, you're tougher than you look. Maybe you're right. I *hope* that you are. But this much I know – the people are beaten and subdued now. It'll take something special to rouse them. Conhain was one of a kind."

Lanrik roused himself. "You're right," he said. He wiped tears from his face. "And there'll never be another like him. But his deeds are part of each of us. We remember his courage, his loyalty, and most of all, we remember his self-sacrifice. And when the time comes, Ebona will find that there are thousands of Conhains in this city, because there's a little of him in all of us."

Bragga Mor sat back. "Well, I wish you luck. I wish us all luck. There's truth to what you say. But that time, if and when it comes, isn't today. Today, a philosopher died, and no one helped him. Least of all me. Panic runs through the streets. Today is a day to keep your head down and to stay out of trouble. Tomorrow … we shall see."

The bard stood. He shook both their hands.

"Good luck," he said. "I don't know what you plan to do, and it's best that way. Who knows? One day I might sing lays about you." He shrugged. "Or perhaps elegies."

He turned and left.

When he was gone, Lanrik glanced at Erlissa. "So, that was Bragga Mor. I've always wanted to meet him. A pity that he only had bad news."

"I get the feeling that good news is rare in the city these days. But we have to carry on. So, what's next?"

Lanrik looked at her steadily. He had already made up his mind.

"We have to see the body. Is it really the Lindrath, or is it just another rumor?"

Erlissa met his gaze without surprise. "I thought that's what you'd say. I really don't think it's a rumor, though. Bragga Mor was certain."

"So he was, and I believe him, but we have to check before we can move ahead with anything else. Besides, we need to see the palace too. I want find out how well guarded it is."

They went to leave the shop. The waitress bowed to them, and Lanrik tried to pay, but she refused.

"It's already on Bragga Mor's account," she explained.

They left, and stepped back onto the Hainer Lon. It was crowded, and there were still signs of unrest, but the panic after the killing had lessened.

They moved quickly down the street. Noon had come and gone, but the city remained busy. It was a good time to go to the palace, for the crowds would offer them concealment. After verifying the Lindrath's death, they would then have to find a place to spend the night, and to work out what to do next.

They retraced their steps, passing the Merenloth again. Royal Guards stood at its entrance, and Lanrik and Erlissa walked on the other side of the street in order to keep the crowd between them and any watchful eyes.

The guards did not pay them any interest. They seemed intent only on ensuring that nobody went inside. Lanrik wondered if the queen would close it permanently. That would serve little real purpose, but it would reinforce that she was in control, and that she did not tolerate dissent.

They moved ahead, passing through an area that they had not seen this morning. Earlier, they had skirted the central part of the city. Now, they headed right into it.

There were dangers in what they were doing, but truly nowhere was safe for them. And they *must* confirm that the Lindrath was dead. Alive, he could be pivotal in trying to defeat Ebona, serving as a rally point for the people. He was famed. And loved. Not least, Lanrik thought, by himself.

The street felt somehow unfamiliar to him, even though he had been this way countless times. Esgallien was his home, but there was little joy here now. The people he loved were dead, and nothing was left of happiness but memories.

He wondered, when all of this was over one day, if he could ever face living here again. He put the thought aside. It was something to consider in the future, if he had one. For the present, he was the new Lindrath, and even if his Raithlin served all of Alithoras, Esgallien was still a part of it.

They entered the inner district. Erlissa walked quietly beside him. Her presence was a comfort, and no words were needed. She knew what he was going through, and she was there for him.

They trod footpaths tiled with colored mosaics. All about them were signs of wealth. The buildings rose high, and their bricks were faced with marble. Many had peaked and decorative roofs, or even towers, and bright flags fluttered from high poles signaling the names of famous people or the houses of the nobility.

On their right, they passed the Haranast. It was still open, and people crowded it. A dull roar washed into the street. A race was going on, and somewhere far out of sight, down on the bottom of the sand-covered arena, horses were galloping. People cheered them on. He pictured it easily, for he had been a member of that crowd many times himself. Would they be cheering if they knew what had happened earlier in the Merenloth?

The Merenloth was a different kind of place, though. It was built for singing, speaking and debates. The Haranast was somewhere that people had fun, and drank. He doubted the Witch-queen would close it, as she seemed to have done with the Merenloth. That would only give the population free time to think on all the wrongs that she had perpetuated, and perhaps to act on their grievances. She would rather distract them.

Soon they came to the Karlenthern. It was quiet today. He remembered it as the place where Lathmai had won the archery tournament in the Spring Games. That was a good memory, but he could not think of it without picturing how she had died. Truly, Esgallien was full of memories, and the good and the bad had all become one.

"We're getting close," Erlissa said.

It was true. The palace was nearby, situated on the edge of Conhain Court. The closer he got, the less he wanted to continue. He did not wish to see the Lindrath. Not dead, anyway. It would be another memory to haunt him. He had seen too many dead people already – those he loved, and those that circumstance had forced him to kill. He did not want to see more, but he knew he must.

There would be Royal Guards ahead. This was near their barracks, for their primary purpose was to protect the kings and queens of Esgallien and the palace. It would be dangerous soon, and he wished that he could get rid of Erlissa's staff. But he could not, and in truth, many people in Esgallien carried one. Bodyguards were common, and the staff was a weapon of choice for many who could not afford swords.

"Conhain Court," he said to Erlissa. "Are you ready?"

She looked ahead. "Let's get this over with."

They moved ahead. The Hainer Lon merged into the great square. It would start again on the other side, but here, in the heart of the city, there was no road, only a mass of people.

There was something about the court that always inspired Lanrik. It was huge, colonnaded on all sides, and scattered throughout it were bronze statues of Esgallien's kings and queens: some mounted for hunting or war. Some with their crowns and royal regalia. Some that were serious. Some that beamed cheerfully. But all of them were part of the deep history of the city. None more so than Conhain. He sat astride his great warhorse, suffering and determination etched by the sculptor into his every feature. In one hand, he held high the famous Red Cloth of Victory.

Through gaps in the crowd Lanrik saw into the center of the square and glimpsed the large platform situated there. It was a place of ceremony, but also where he had fought Mecklar in the sword tournament of the Spring Games. Yet another memory that bubbled to the surface. At least, there was not going to be a fight today. Guards or no guards, it should be easy enough to see the Lindrath's body, to pay some last respects, and to get out of there. Tomorrow was another day, and that would be soon enough to work out what to do next.

They moved through the crowds. The court seemed as busy as ever, and though everything appeared as it normally did: the markets, the seething mass of pedestrians, the noise and carrying on, he did notice that there were more armed people than usual. He should have realized this earlier. It was common enough for someone to carry a sword, and many carried staffs, but it seemed now that every second person bore a weapon. And they were watchful, too.

"It seems so normal," Erlissa said. "And yet, there's a look to the people. They're scared. I get the feeling that they could break into a panic at any moment, and for little reason."

What she said was true. These people would feel safer here than elsewhere, because there was protection in numbers, and yet even here they did not feel secure. It showed in all the weapons, their furtive glances, and the distance they kept from one another. Most of all, it showed in the lack of playing children. Normally, the court would be full of them, but he saw only adults now.

Erlissa nudged him and pointed. "I wonder what she would think of all this?"

They had come to Rhodmai's statue. Here, she was crowned and wore all her royal regalia, and yet she had the same cheery face as shown on the paintings in the Bridge Inn.

"It wouldn't have happened in her time," he said.

Erlissa nodded. "No. Lòhrens were welcome. And kind old lady that she was, she would have made sure that Ebona never entered the city, never gained a following, and never had a chance to influence anything, let alone rule. Murhain has a lot to answer for."

So he did, but Lanrik suddenly wondered if even the king now feared for his life. Had he realized his mistake? Could he perhaps even be counted an ally in defeating Ebona? He did not think so, but it was something to consider.

He remembered Aranloth's prophecy that the king would come to a bad end. Well, that was likely enough. Certainly, when the queen was defeated, he would be in trouble. The people would no longer tolerate him after what he had allowed to happen.

But Murhain did not have any heirs. Who would be crowned in his place? All that was left of the royal family were distant relatives. None of them really had a stronger claim than the others, and none were particularly competent. The true blood of Conhain's line had grown thin, and none now living matched their ancestor. But a strong leader would be needed when Ebona was gone, for the realm was always at risk from its enemies in the south. An elug army, led by a new shazrahad, could come at any time.

They moved across the square. At its end, on the right hand side, was a separate colonnade that led to the front of the palace. They neared it now, and he walked ever more slowly.

"Careful," he said. "From here on there could be guards."

They walked down the colonnade. There were less people here. Ahead, the palace rose up, a stately building, surrounded by its own court, grassed areas and gardens. But all that was fenced off. Metal pickets, black, sharp-spiked and tall, surrounded it.

At the end of the colonnade stood a massive wrought-iron gate. He saw no guards, which was strange. Normally, there were two here. But the gate was closed, as was usual, for it served only as a ceremonial entry into the palace grounds during times of pomp and celebration. A smaller gate, far to the right, was the usual entry for day-to-day use.

They approached, and he saw the body. As Bragga Mor had said, it was chained to the gate. There were only a few people here, and they hurried past without looking.

They walked ahead. Lanrik's heart began to thud. He did not want to do this, for he already had memories of Lathmai that he could not erase, though the images of her burnt and broken body haunted his sleep less often than they used to. If he saw the tortured body of the Lindrath, it would stay with him just as long.

Erlissa held his hand, and they proceeded. There was no one near them now. He smelled a hint of decay. Soon, a stench would cloy the air and reach even into Conhain Court. His gaze traced rivulets of blood along several of the gate-bars, now caked dry. A black pool, semi-congealed and swarming with flies, marred the cobbles.

He made himself look up. The Lindrath hung there, chained roughly by his neck to the top of the gate. His arms and body drooped motionless. The Raithlin cloak, worn with pride throughout his life, was become a tattered and dirty rag, rent in a dozen places by knife or sword, soiled by dirt, blood and vomit.

A slow rage welled up inside Lanrik. It rose, like a living thing, and it swirled with feelings of hatred, retribution and a yearning to destroy those who had done this. He pushed it down, for he sensed his self-control slipping, and that would not serve the Lindrath, or Esgallien. But he would not forget.

"He fought them," Erlissa said unexpectedly. "See the wounds to his arms and legs? They're not torture marks. They were caused by fending off attacks. And see his knuckles? They're red. He landed several blows at least, before they took him."

It was something. The Lindrath would have defied them as long as possible. But no man could endure the pain that he must have without breaking. His eyes were gone, plucked from their sockets. His face bashed. Black bruises blossomed over most of his skin like a creeping disease. And fire, or red-hot bars, had seared him. The skin of his face, peeled and blackened, still oozed blood from sickly blisters.

Lanrik closed his eyes. It did not help. Instead of the Lindrath, he saw Lathmai. She too had suffered the unendurable. He felt the rage inside him rise again.

"Is that his seal?" Erlissa asked.

Lanrik did not answer. He looked at the Lindrath's ring. He had seen it often enough. It was a band of gold, embossed with the Raithlin motif of a trotting fox looking back over its shoulder. They had left him that, and no thief had dared steal it. Strange that it remained, though. He supposed Ebona would want people to see it, to know that it was the Lindrath. And yet, the body had been here for two days. There were no guards, at least at the moment. Some desperate thief would have removed it by now, unless Ebona kept a closer watch than was apparent. He felt suddenly uneasy, and looked around.

There was no one near except for passersby, moving through with their eyes down. And yet, there were shops not that far away. Guards could be stationed inside them, and he would not see them.

"Are you satisfied that it's the Lindrath?" Erlissa asked.

"It looks like him. The hair is right, and his build. And it *is* his seal, too. But his face is so badly beaten. It has to be him, and yet…"

"And yet?"

"Something isn't right."

Erlissa did not answer. She let him continue to think, and his gaze scrutinized the corpse. It made him feel sick. The face was unrecognizable, so he concentrated on other parts of the body. The hands seemed right. They were long fingered and tanned from the sun. The arms were lean but well muscled from years of sword craft. His gaze strayed to the ring again. It was the final confirmation that it was the Lindrath, the best that he would ever have, but something disturbed him. Badly.

"Erlissa?"

"Yes?"

"There's no scar on the back of his thumb."

"Did he have one?"

"Yes. Very faint, but it was there."

Erlissa peered closely. "I don't see one. How do you even know it was there?"

"Because I gave it to him. He was showing me some knife-fighting techniques. I got carried away, and drew blood. He wasn't happy with me that day … but the scar was permanent."

Erlissa straightened. "But if it's not him, what would be the point of hanging a body here? And we know that he was captured. Bragga Mor confirmed it. Why hold him prisoner, but try to trick people into thinking he was dead?"

Lanrik looked away from the corpse and straight at her.

"What if he escaped before she had a chance to kill him? That was one of the rumors. Bragga Mor said that, too."

Her eyes widened. "Is it possible?"

Lanrik was about to answer, but then he smelled something out of place.

"Smoke!" he said.

Erlissa sniffed the air. "I smell it. There's something wrong here, Lan. Very wrong."

She tilted her head, and frowned in concentration.

"I sense something else, too. There's more than smoke. I feel sorcery."

They looked about them. They saw nothing. And then the acrid odor grew suddenly stronger. A movement of light flickered in the doorway of one of the shops.

"Is the building on fire?" he asked.

Erlissa's eyes narrowed.

"No!" she yelled. "Something inside is burning. And it's moving!"

One moment Lanrik hesitated when he should have run. One moment only, but in those few seconds many things happened.

Royal Guards sprinted toward them from several shops. Brinhain was among them. And with him was a creature of nightmare. A man who burned. A man whose eyes flickered with light and brimmed with need.

The creature lurched toward them. Guards came from left and right. Lanrik turned, looking back through the colonnade to Conhain Court. Guards filled it as well.

"We're surrounded!" he said.

8. Defiance

Erlissa spun around. "My staff!"

Lanrik passed it to her, and deftly drew his sword. They were not without defenses, and yet their enemies were many. They could not hold them off for long.

He prepared for a last stand; one that they must ensure killed them, for death was better than being taken alive to the Witch-queen.

Erlissa surprised him by stepping forward. A moment she stood, poised and still, as their enemies rushed toward them. And then with a sudden flick of the tip of her staff, a blue flame sprang upward from the cobbles. It burned coldly in an arc, reaching to the fence on either side.

The fire flickered, growing taller, turning and twisting in a way that drew the eye. Lanrik ignored it. His gaze was on the enemy. He watched them through the blue haze as they gathered on its far side.

The lòhrengai would not last long; that much he understood instantly. He cast his gaze around again, trying to find a way out. The only place where there were no guards was behind them, and that was because the gate and fence formed an impassable barrier.

In desperation, he turned to the gate and shook it. It barely moved. The guards had made sure it was locked. But his seeking eyes glimpsed something of use.

The corpse hung there, but it swayed with the force of his shaking. A great loop of chain, coming down from where it was wrapped over the high crossbar of the gate, swung into view from behind the body. He pulled it through the bars to his own side.

"Erlissa!" he yelled.

She was by his side in a moment.

"Climb!"

She did not hesitate. Handing him her staff, she grasped the chain in her hands and braced her feet against one of the thick bars. She climbed, reaching the top quickly.

She looked uncomfortable as she negotiated the spikes, but used the chain to cover as many as she could. Spots of blood blossomed on her clothes. Fabric was torn. She gasped with effort or pain, and then she was over the top and able to drop to the ground on the other side.

Lanrik took a quick look behind him. The blue flames were already dying, and the guards had moved closer. They left space for the charred-man, though. Lanrik caught another glimpse of his eyes. Human eyes, filled with torment and a frantic need to catch his prey.

He sheathed his sword and climbed the gate. The heavy chain smashed into iron bars and rattled as he hastened. The corpse swayed grotesquely, and then he landed lightly on the other side.

He did not feel any damage from the iron spikes until he caught a glimpse of blood on his arms and legs. After that, his injuries throbbed. But they were only superficial and would not slow him.

For a quick moment he thought about where to go. They were inside the palace grounds now, and there were sure to be guards. But at least they would not already be chasing them as the others were.

They raced off. He veered a little toward the right, across the cobbles and then onto lawn. They made quick time, but swift as they were, their lead was short. Guards had jumped the dying lòhrengai and used the chain as he had. Even the charred-man now lurched toward them. He ran strangely, tilting from side to side, twisting and turning as he moved. And yet for all that, he kept pace with the guards.

"The trees!" Erlissa called.

It was a good idea. They changed direction slightly, and headed toward a grove of oaks. They were ancient things, and it was dark beneath them. Here, they veered again and followed a gravel-lined path. They saw nobody now, and yet the pursuit must still be close. Even so, without seeing where their quarry went, the guards might split up to take different routes through the grove, or go around it altogether.

After a hundred paces or so they were out of the grove and onto grass again. Now, they were near the palace. It rose before them, grand and elegant. There were people here, courtiers of some sort, and palace servants. They watched as he and Erlissa raced past them, but made no move to interfere.

He heard a call from the grove and looked back. A group of guards burst from it, yelling to attract the attention of the others. The charred-man was among them, and if he could somehow track them by sorcery, or if they were just unlucky, Lanrik did not know.

They sped down the right-hand side of the palace. There was a cobbled path here, and their boots slammed loudly against its hard surface. A horn screeched from somewhere inside, blown as an alert of some kind to warn of intruders.

There were sure to be more guards on the chase now. And then he saw something that chilled his blood. Whether looking because of the blowing horn, or because she sensed the presence of her own sorcery in the form of the charred-man nearing, Ebona was there.

The witch leaned over a high balcony, her hard gaze on them, and hatred evident in her stiff posture. And yet she must be too far away to attempt any attack of her own. She watched them race past, her body taut beneath her plain white dress, and in moments they passed from view and came to the back of the palace.

They crossed another court. It was small, and decorative statues filled it. He had never been here before. It seemed like a miniature version of Conhain Court. They raced among the statues. Other horns blew now, and then a company of guards trotted from a doorway on the ground floor of the palace.

"More of them!" he said.

Erlissa did not answer him. She was panting for breath, as was he. He knew this could not go on much longer. They needed to hide, for they could not outrun such a chase for long – not with new guards, fresh to the pursuit, taking it up.

They sped right over the top of some flowerbeds. A gardener, hoe in hand, watched them race by. He made no move to stop them, though he saw the guards following. He dropped the hoe and disappeared into a nearby grove of trees.

Ahead was the opposite side of the palace fence. They reached it, and then raced along its length. There should be a gate somewhere near, though it too would be guarded. They soon saw what they were looking for, and the guards that they expected. There were only two of them though, even if they were alert. One watched out toward the city, the other looked in, scrutinizing the palace grounds. He said something to his companion, who turned. They unsheathed their swords and waited.

Lanrik did not slow. In a quick motion he drew one knife, and then another. He hurled them at the guards.

His aim was a little off, for running and throwing was difficult, but it forced the men to duck, and then he was among them, kicking and punching. A sword clattered to the ground. There was a thump as Erlissa struck one of the guards in the head with her staff. In a moment, they were through.

They ran from the palace grounds into the city, but several of the pursuing guards were close behind. Panic spread in the people-filled streets. Screams cut the air when the charred-man lumbered through the gate.

Darting left and right down a series of wide streets they tried to lose their pursuers. But they were a clear target, easily seen, and the crowd was not so thick as to get in the way of the guards.

"There!" shouted Lanrik.

He turned into the first narrow street that he could find. It was not an alley, but perhaps if they followed it they would find a shop with a back door or some other means of escape.

It was a place that he knew fairly well, having been here many times, and then he remembered that somewhere to the right was a narrow lane between two grand buildings. He found it and turned, but heard pursuers close behind.

He headed into the lane, and it was as he remembered. But a dozen people cluttered it, and a cart blocked the way forward. It was a manure wagon, wide and low to the ground. It barely fit in the alley, and to pass by on either side was impossible. The only way was over it.

The horse that pulled it was no longer yoked. Someone had led it a little way forward while people worked on the cart. It seemed that a wheel was damaged, but it was impossible to access from the side.

Lanrik did not care. There was only one way out, and that was over the top. Everyone looked at the two of them as they dashed forward, and then beyond them. Lanrik heard noises behind him, and turned to look. The guards had caught up.

"Go!" he yelled to Erlissa.

He drew his sword and faced the enemy. They raced at him. He cut and thrust, deflected and sliced, and in a mist of blood three guards lay dead. His sword dripped red, and the crowd behind him was shocked to complete silence.

He looked ahead. More guards rounded the corner into the lane. Brinhain was among them.

"Kill them!" the captain screamed, and the guards padded forward carefully, blades held high.

Erlissa was suddenly by his side. "We're in this together, Lanrik. And when the charred-man comes, you'll need me."

He wanted to argue, but did not. Nothing would change her mind. He thought of calling for help from the people on the far side of the cart, asking them to take her away, but he knew she would resist.

He flicked the blood from his sword and held the tip at eye-level. He would meet the guards with death, and perhaps give Erlissa another opportunity to escape, when she saw that it was necessary. But something unexpected happened.

He heard murmuring behind him. It was faint at first, and then grew loud. He caught the word *Raithlin* several times, before it was shouted. The crowd had seen the etching on his blade.

The guards came on. Surprisingly, the crowd edged forward, rather than away, and there was hope in their faces.

They wanted him to win. But he could not. Not against so many. He was about to beg Erlissa to go, and then the charred-man appeared. It lurched ahead of the guards, who now held back.

Erlissa took a step forward. "Go!" she said. This is a creature beyond you."

He shook his head and repeated her own words. "We're in this together."

The creature lurched down the street at them. Its feverish eyes flickered with anticipation, but then it came to a stop. Its whole body shuddered, and like a dog shaking water from its coat, it flung fire at them.

Bright flame sizzled through the air. Erlissa raised her staff, and a wall of blue light, cold like ice, formed a shield in front of them. The fire of the charred-man struck it. Sparks flew and hissed like a swarm of wasps.

With a puff of blue smoke the two opposing flames disappeared. Erlissa did not hesitate. She leveled her staff and lòhren-fire shot from its tip. It smashed into the charred-man and sent him sprawling.

Lanrik's heart thumped. Erlissa was growing as a lòhren, and though her power was slight compared to Aranloth, clearly she was a force to be reckoned with. And yet, as quick as hope was born, it died.

The charred-man stood. It shrugged, and blue flame cascaded from its body to the cobbles. The cracks between the stone bricks steamed as moisture was drawn from beneath them.

Their attacker stepped forward, unharmed, perhaps even looking stronger, and Lanrik realized that lòhren-fire held no power over it.

Most of the crowd had now fled, but some brave souls continued to watch. Panicked cries rose from among them, and yet one man, bearded and tall called out in a deep voice.

"Tip the cart!" he said, and those left followed his instructions.

Erlissa seemed at a loss. She kept her staff leveled and gazed at the creature intently, while it in turn inched forward cautiously. Neither seemed willing to give ground.

Lanrik glanced back at the cart. The crowd had tipped it forward, and manure piled out onto the lane. Most of the wagon now rested atop its former load, but one side leaned against a brick wall.

He saw his chance, and understood what the bearded man had done. There was now a gap, small, but enough to allow a quick escape.

He grabbed Erlissa by the arm. "Run!" he said.

He pushed her through the gap, and then scrambled through himself.

What was left of the crowd dispersed, realizing that the fight would now come to them. Even the bearded man disappeared, running swiftly around a corner.

Once on the other side of the cart they turned. The charred-man ran toward them, scores of guards now hanging back behind it. Erlissa raised her staff. Fire burst from its tip, and she sent it flying into the cart. The timber planks that formed its tray caught alight. Straw and manure smoldered. In moments, the cart blazed with flame, no longer the blue of her lòhrengai, but natural tones.

A wave of heat sent them staggering back, and the air shimmered.

"That should slow them," Lanrik said. He turned to run, but Erlissa hesitated. He turned back again.

"It'll slow the men," she said. "But not it!"

Through the billowing flames he saw what she meant. The charred-man had begun to move through the gap between the cart and the brick wall. It moved with its usual lurching gait, seemingly unaffected by the flames.

Without a further word they turned and fled. In moments, they heard the uneven tread of their pursuer pound the cobbles behind them.

9. Separation

They sped through streets. The people nearby shot them curious looks; but their intrigued expressions soon turned to ones of fear when the charred-man lumbered into view. And for all his monstrous lurching and twitching, he ran at a fast and steady pace.

"Doesn't it tire?" Lanrik gasped.

Erlissa glanced over her shoulder. "Ebona's witchery sustains it."

Lanrik thought about that as they ran. It was clear that Erlissa's lòhrengai was not of a type that could readily defeat this thing. The Witch-queen had brought it into being with an understanding of the knowledge and talents possessed by its prey. Erlissa, on the other hand, knew nothing of it, and she was forced to try to find a way to defeat it even as she fled for her life. It was a disadvantage that she might not have the time to overcome.

He glanced back. The creature had gained on them, and he came to a decision.

"Erlissa!" he called out. "We can't out run it. And we can't get far enough ahead to hide."

She looked at him with wide eyes. Her chest heaved as she gasped for air, but she gave no reply.

"We have to separate," he said.

"No!" she answered. "I'll think of something."

"We don't have enough time. It'll wear us down in a few more minutes." He gulped more air before he spoke again. "It's the only way. At least one of us will survive. Otherwise, it'll catch us both together."

"No! I won't!" Erlissa said.

"We're dead if we don't. And our hopes for Esgallien with us."

She shook her head, but looked back at the charred-man again. The expression on her face showed that she saw what he had. It was gaining on them.

"We must!" he called out. He saw her anguish and doubt.

They ran a little further, and he gave her the time she needed to recognize the necessity of his plan.

"At the next intersection," she replied. "I'll go left. You go right."

She understood, even if she hated the idea. His lungs burned like they were on fire, and he felt his legs begin to go wobbly from strain. But he was determined to go on. The race was not yet over, and he intended the finish line to be one of his own making.

"If we can, we'll meet again near the stables in the Haranast," he offered.

They both knew this was unlikely. He saw by her expression that she felt one of them was likely to die. And she was right. It only firmed his resolve for what he had already planned.

They neared the intersection. He reached out and squeezed her shoulder. He caught a fleeting glimpse of her eyes. They brimmed with worry and thoughts that could never be put into words. A swift moment of understanding passed between them. All that they were, all that they might never get the chance to become, was laid bare.

The moment passed, and then they were at the intersection. An instant longer they looked, and then they separated. She sped to the left, and he to the right. But he slowed and looked behind him.

The creature was closing rapidly. Lanrik came to a stop and drew his sword. He waited until the charred-man veered in his direction, and then, now sure that it would pursue him, he sheathed it and ran again. *One of them had to live. It would be her.*

Fear breathed new life into his legs. The creature was very close now, and he sensed it straining behind him. It made no noise as it ran though. All that he heard was the heavy slapping of its smoldering boots over cobbles.

Screams rose all about him. He ignored them, and a sense of accomplishment settled deep inside him. Every second that he delayed this thing, every footstep that it must spend following him, was a greater chance that Erlissa might live. And Esgallien needed her more than him. She knew the goings on in the city, just the same as he did. Most of all, she knew of the Lindrath's escape and survival. If they found him, he was the key that Aranloth might use to rouse the people against the Witch-queen, and between them all, and the other lòhrens, they could challenge Ebona's hold over the city.

There was little that he could contribute to that, and he knew it. But that did not mean he intended to just lay down and die. He would soon find out if the charred-man was as immune to cold steel as he was to fire.

He ran on. The thing was behind him, but his burst of speed had given him a little lead again. They reached the Hainer Lon once more. There was even less chance of escaping it here. He veered away as soon as he could, and raced down a side street at random. One destination was as good as another, so long as it gave Erlissa more time.

He was nearly ready to turn and confront his pursuer, for he wanted to conserve enough strength to ensure he put up a good fight. He had no illusions though that he would necessarily be able to bring his sword to bear. The charred-man might simply fling fire at him as it had done earlier. If that happened, he had no defense.

Something occurred to him then. A steel blade was a good weapon against most things, though he feared it might not serve him now. But the idea of cold steel brought to mind water. What if he could find a fountain? Would it offer him protection of any kind? It was possible, even if unlikely.

He tried to think, but there was no water nearby. Esgallien's many parks contained a large number of fountains and ponds, but the closest one was too far away. The charred-man would catch up with him before he reached it.

He ran only a few paces more before he cursed himself for a fool. There *was* water nearby. He just had not thought of it.

When he came to the next corner he turned, ran a little down that street, and then doubled back toward the Hainer Lon. The creature doggedly kept on his trail, and fury burned once more in his heart. He did not like being hunted. It was on his mind to turn and fight, and damn the consequences, and yet there was one last chance for him, one last thing to try before it came to that.

He drew near the Hainer Lon again. He knew this part of the city well, and ran quickly beneath a portico to his left. People screamed and fled, as they had done all along, and just as always, the charred-man ignored them in its single-minded pursuit.

But it was time to mix things up and to see what effect, if any, a change of environment had on it.

Lanrik ran up a few stairs and into the doorway of a building. Here, there were few people inside, but those who were quickly scattered.

He raced across the marble floor, and the creature followed his trail like a hunting dog on the scent.

100

Dashing onto a stairwell, he ran down it. It soon became quite dim, and for once he opened a gap between him and the creature. Its lurching gate was ill-suited to stairs, and that was something Lanrik noted; it might come in handy. But for now, he had another plan.

He flung open some wooden doors and went into a kind of basement. He knew this building particularly well, but it was possible that things had changed since he was last here.

This was a building used by Esgallien's tax collectors. And as with many government structures, the Raithlin had access to them. They used them in their training, for there were times that a suitable situation in the wild could not be found, or was too far away to be of practical use. If they wanted to practice certain skills, they had to make do with what was around them.

He saw what he wanted. There was a narrow grill on the far wall. It was an old thing of rusted iron, a thing that he had seen many times before. It led into a tunnel beneath the Hainer Lon. But it was no ordinary tunnel. It was an aqueduct that fed water to the entire city. The Raithlin used it as though it was a cave, and practiced a whole set of skills there that they could not elsewhere.

The aqueduct started high in the wild hills just to the west of Esgallien. Somewhere up there in ancient times a spring had been diverted from its normal course. Clean water ran through an underground channel of tightly-fitted bricks, winding ever-downward to the city.

It finally reached River Gate, and continuing its underground path it passed along the full length of the Hainer Lon, before emptying into Esgallien Creek. The whole city drew water from it.

Many wells were in government buildings, which were also places of access for the workmen who checked for leaks and contamination. And those places of access were also once used by the Raithlin. He looked at one now, unless it had been closed since the disbanding of the Raithlin. He reached it, and pulled hard on the iron grid. Nothing happened.

A cold echo sounded in the confines of the basement, and he knew that the charred-man had arrived.

10. A Wilderness of Dark

The grid did not budge. Sudden panic drove Lanrik to pull with all his strength. Still, nothing happened.

He saw the problem immediately. The ends of the grid's bars were now fixed behind a layer of bricks, whereas before they had merely butted up against the sides of the recess. Access to the aqueduct was closed off. And yet all that the workmen had done was remove the material that was already there, set the grid deeper into the alcove, and then re-mortar the bricks in place.

Behind him, the charred-man approached. Lanrik drew his sword, but he did not turn to face the creature. He made one last attempt to open the way forward.

Swiftly, he used his blade to provide leverage by wedging it through the bars and using the bricks as a pivot. He heaved again. This time, mortar popped like a fistful of thrown sand, and bricks clattered to the floor. He took hold of the grid in one hand and flung it at the charred-man.

The creature, for all that it could run without cessation, was not nimble. The grid struck it and sent it sprawling, but it clambered to its feet a moment later, seemingly unharmed.

Lanrik did not wait. He sheathed the sword and dived head first through the narrow opening. Instantly, it was dark, but not so dark that it stopped him from seeing.

He rolled to his feet and ran. He knew where he was going, and the small amount of light that filtered down through the opening behind him was enough to make him sure of his bearings. Within a few paces he noticed a lantern on the floor, filled with oil. It was used by the workmen who frequented this place. There was a tinderbox too. He swept them up as he passed, but there was no time to make light.

It grew darker. Behind him, he heard the shuffling gait of the charred-man. Ahead of him, was an ancient stairwell. He moved down it carefully.

At the bottom he turned right. In a moment the passage narrowed, but it soon dropped down at a steep slope into the aqueduct. Water gurgled past. It was a reassuring sound, as though the wilderness had come to the confined space. But it was also quite dark here, and he paused long enough to light the lantern. It would enable the charred-man to follow him, but on the other hand he needed to see where he was going. Light from grills like the one he had come through was too infrequent to rely on, and an accident down here would ensure his death.

The lantern flickered to life, and he closed the shutter so that only a glimmer of light escaped. The aqueduct was tall enough to enable him to walk upright. At this point, it was perhaps ten feet wide, but he knew that varied along its length and he hesitated as to which direction to take.

A breath later, he moved to the right. He had no definite plan, but right or left did not matter. What was important was that he got going.

The water was cold. He tried to keep to the edge of the tunnel, for the floor was of tight-fitting bricks that sloped gently inward to keep the flow in the center of the channel. Yet the depth varied depending upon the rainfall in the hills and the usage of the city. Now, it ran knee high and filled the entire bottom of the passage. Just as well that there had not been recent heavy rain, or he would be wading forward in water above his waist.

The hollow splashing of his pursuer soon sounded loud behind him. He had not expected to lose the charred-man, although he had considered the chance that the creature, a thing of fire as it was, would not follow him into the water. That hope had died, and yet it did seem as though it was slower than above ground. It might have been the water, or the difficulty of keeping footing down here, or both. At any rate, the difference was only slight. It pursued him in the same dogged fashion, and Lanrik wondered if he would be killed here, alone in the dark, his body never to be discovered until workmen came to find and remove the source of contamination from the water. It was a dark thought. He shrugged it off and stepped ahead at a faster pace.

The charred-man stayed with him. They were both quiet, except for the occasional splash of water. Drifting from afar were the sounds of the city: remote, dim and muffled reminders of another world. Above was the Hainer Lon, and for all the fear in the city, compared to this, it was still a place heady with life.

He wondered if he had only succeeded in trapping himself down here with his enemy, and yet it was apparent that though the water did not deter it, it had slowed it just enough that he could catch his breath and allow some of the leaden tiredness to drain from his legs.

Perhaps he was even unlucky that it had not rained in the hills lately. If it had, the deeper water might have slowed the creature even more. Could it even swim? That was a thought. It seemed ungainly, for all its endurance, and so the question was worth asking.

He strode ahead, doubtful that he could run any more even if circumstances allowed. He was tired, tired as he had seldom been before, but a plan was taking shape in the back of his mind.

Far ahead the Hainer Lon ran past a park. It was a large sprawl of tens of acres of gardens, trees and lawns. There were stone benches around little courtyards, shops that sold food and drink, and areas set aside for athletic contests. An offshoot from the aqueduct provided the necessary water to establish plants and keep growing things green and lush. If he could reach that place, where a massive underground cistern stored water for the gardeners, perhaps he could put some of his thoughts to the test.

He had to leave the main branch of the aqueduct somewhere anyway. If he went too far, he would be trapped, for a massive grid closed it off beneath River Gate. Just as nothing came into the city that was not wanted above ground, so it was beneath the surface.

No one knew if Esgallien's enemies had discovered the aqueduct, though it was likely and must be assumed to be the case. In a time of war, deep wells in the city provided a separate water supply on the chance that it was poisoned.

If he somehow managed to get that far, he would either be trapped at the grid, or, finding his way up to the towers above River Gate, run headlong into soldiers. Neither were acceptable options.

The minutes passed. Water squished inside his boots, cold and clammy. His pursuer was relentless as always, a silent thing that did not speak, did not call out in challenge, did not taunt him for running as a normal man might. It just pursued him, without thought or will of its own, in some abhorrent fulfillment of Ebona's witchery.

Once, though, it had been a man, and Ebona had done something to it, something over and above the obvious sorcery. It *must* chase him. That much he understood intuitively. It had no choice, and would never relent, unless he somehow killed it and released it from torment.

He could not hate it. He only wished to find a way to save himself, and, if possible, to undo the wrong that Ebona had perpetrated.

The park was close now. It was hard to tell where he was underground, but he remembered this place, saw more stairwells leading up into other government buildings, and recognized exactly where he was. Soon, the passage leading into the cistern would branch off. He must not miss it. It was a narrow channel at first, easy to pass by unwittingly in the dark, but he could not afford that.

He slowed a little. It should be near, but so too was the charred-man. It no doubt gained a little on him now as he slowed to search for the turnoff, but he could not help that.

With trembling fingers he opened the lantern shutter a little more, shining light on the brick wall. It was surprisingly dry here, although white patches of minerals scudded the walls where running water had flowed at higher levels over the centuries.

At length, he spotted what he wanted, and something else, besides. Since the last time he was here, someone had scraped rough letters on the brickwork. It was hurried writing, but clear enough to read. And, after all, he knew the words well.

> *Our duty is to serve and protect*
> *Our honor is to fight but not hate*
> *Our love is for all that is good in the world*

The Raithlin creed. Strange to find it here, and yet perhaps his comrades had sought refuge in the aqueduct when the Witch-queen persecuted them, even as he did now. If so, she had found them here, that much was certain. But it must have served them for a time, and that gave him hope.

He turned right into the narrow channel and reflected on the creed's values. Who did he now serve? What was his honor? These things had altered recently, as steadfastly as he had always believed in them. Once, he had thought that they would last a lifetime. That reminded him of Conhain. *Nothing lasts forever.*

He went ahead, but soon heard the splashing of the creature behind him. It had found the turn and followed him, as he expected it would. The flow of water was lesser here, for it was only a side channel, and yet the reservoir ahead was large – if he could reach it. But the charred-man had changed pace. It gained on him, or he had slowed down too much. Either way, a fluttering fear ran through him once more and he hurried ahead in the darkness.

It was a nightmarish chase, alone and unaided, with nothing more than the thought that Raithlin had once used these tunnels to keep him company. And yet they had not given up, and nor would he.

At length, he saw light ahead: there were many grills and wells where gardeners dropped buckets into the cistern to collect water.

He came to a sudden stop. Just before him, he saw the reservoir. It was an underground lake, its bottom no doubt lined by mud, its surface still, and perhaps ten to twenty feet of clear water between the two.

With a flick of his fingers he shuttered the lantern and cast it behind him in the dark. The shuffling splash of the creature paused a moment, and then continued. It was even closer than he thought.

He stood on the edge of a little waterfall. The water dropped off the ledge and down onto the cistern below.

It was a long drop, but Lanrik did not hesitate. He plunged, feet first, and sent up a hope for good luck to whoever looked after fools and Raithlins. Or both.

He smashed into the cold water and went right under. Water pressed at his ears and his eyes and his mouth, and then he bobbed up again, gasping for fresh air. He struck out for the middle of the reservoir.

Swimming was hard going in all his clothes and with his waterlogged boots, but the Raithlin trained for such circumstances, and he persevered. His broad-brimmed hat was gone though, lost in the dark and soon to sink to the bottom and oblivion.

He reached the center of the reservoir. Bright light shone in his eyes from an opening straight above, but that did not dazzle him so much that he could not see his pursuer.

The charred-man stood just where he had a few moments ago. It twitched and shrugged on the precipice, looking down at him. Lanrik could even see its eyes, dark things that flickered with fiery need, and he wondered if even this last effort to throw it off the chase would work.

11. The Old Lady

Erlissa sprinted ahead.

She expected to hear the lurching tread of the charred-man at any moment. That it would pursue her, rather than Lanrik, she had no doubt. Otherwise, she would have stayed with him.

It was a creature of witchery, brought into existence for one reason: to kill them. And yet her possession of lòhrengai singled her out. Ebona hated lòhrens. More than that, after their confrontation in Caladhrist, she was herself a target of that same personal malice that the witch honed against Aranloth.

And yet the screams around her faded.

She swung her gaze wildly from side to side, nearly stumbling. The people nearby showed no sign of fear. They merely looked at her in annoyance, as though wondering what was wrong with her. Nor did she hear any sound of pursuit.

She risked a look over her shoulder and saw nothing. Nothing that mattered, anyway. She came to a sudden stop and stood there, bent over and panting in the street while people stepped past and gave her furtive looks. Their expressions said that she was an idiot.

Lanrik was gone. The creature was gone. She felt empty inside, and Aranloth's advice came back to her. *Stay together.* If he ever learned what she had just done, he would surely think her an idiot, too.

Closing her eyes, she suppressed the sobbing that threatened to overtake her. It would not make anyone feel better but herself. She steeled her mind, opened her eyes and began to retrace her steps. It was no good running. Lanrik and the creature were gone, and she could not find them unless she heard screams from the crowd. But there was none of that.

She wandered the streets a while longer, desperate to find Lanrik, but to no avail. She saw one of the Royal Guards, and throwing caution to the wind in a fit of anger, ignored him. But soon there were more, and she knew the search for Lanrik, and the creature that must surely kill him, was over.

It was time to take thought for Esgallien. She *was* a lòhren. She would *act* like one. Time enough to cry later, when it did not matter.

Soon, there were even more guards, and against her will she turned her mind to thinking of a way to disguise herself better. She now carried the staff. It was not a common thing for a woman to use, though she was not the only one. From time to time old women as well as men used one to help them walk.

Her description would be circulating through the city. At any moment she could be stopped in the street. Every time a group of guards passed her, she walked slowly, as though she did not have a care in the world, and put the crowd between herself and them. But soon one of the guards that had seen her near the palace would recognize her, and then she would be dead.

The first thing she needed to do was to get off the street and give herself time to think and work through her feelings. She came to the Hainer Lon, a dangerous place for her, although the crowd offered even better concealment. Walking carefully, with the staff held upright against her body, she could almost hide its presence.

Soon, she found a place to hide. It was a sweetshop. She sat down at a table near the back of the room and ordered some of her favorite seed cakes. They were strongly flavored and nutty, bound together and sweetened by wild honey and dusted with exotic spices. She ate one quickly, and then another. They tasted good, and yet she paid them little heed. Her mood was too bleak to enjoy anything, but the everyday activity settled her and provided a chance to sort out her feelings.

She knew at once which one was strongest. Guilt. For some reason, the charred-man had gone after Lanrik. She did not know why, but she should have anticipated it and not separated. And yet remorse would not help him now. She must assume that he was dead, though the thought sent a stab through her heart. But she hardened herself. If he was dead, it was partly her fault, and she would have to live with that, if she could. But for the moment Esgallien needed her, and she must fulfill her mission regardless of how she felt.

And though she must assume that he was lost, a part of her did not, would not ever, give up hope. He was resourceful. He had nearly died many times since she had first met him, and yet somehow he always found a way to survive. He might do so again.

She remembered the first time that she had seen him, a dark figure in the deep shadows of the shazrahad's tent. He had defied a whole army, infiltrated it, got her out of their grasp and taken the commander's prized sword with him. No, her heart would not give up on him, even if her head had.

Her next step must be to go to the Haranast where he had said to meet. He just *might* show. Though she knew that if he did not, a part of her would remain there for the rest of her life, waiting...

She ate another cake. Money was no issue; Aranloth had given them both plenty of coin to get by. The lòhrens kept a store of all the currencies of Alithoras.

She put her mind to another question. How could she walk the streets, avoid guards, and get safely to the Haranast?

Nothing came to her, but she must think harder. She was a lòhren, was she not? She had to find a way. She *would* find a way. Temporarily, she was distracted by a troop of guards that marched down the street. She caught glimpses of their hard faces and seeking eyes from the back of the shop.

The crowd hushed as they passed. The place had been full of idle chatter, and yet it dimmed quickly when the guards came into view. Just as quickly, it bubbled up again when they were gone.

Without a doubt, they were looking for her. They would find her too, if she did not come up with something. But her thoughts kept straying to Lanrik. He no longer carried the shazrahad sword, imbued as it was with Aranloth's lòhrengai. It was the only way he could have protected himself against the charred-man, but he had left that in Lòrenta. And for good reason. It attracted trouble to him like flowers drew bees.

She had a feeling that Aranloth's real purpose in traveling to the Graèglin Dennath had something to do with that, and the mysterious prophecy that was behind it all. Certainly, he intended to fulfill his promise to Ebona, and yet where else could he get information on the sword better than in the land where it was forged? Even if that was dangerous.

She forced herself to focus on her own problems. She knew the city as well as the guards. How could she hide in a place where everyone might be either looking for her, or willing to turn her over to those who were? What did Lanrik often say? The best place to hide was in plain sight. That was such a Raithlin sentiment. Such a *Lanrik* sentiment. But how could she put it into practice? What was the opposite of what Ebona would expect her to do? She must go back onto the street. Yes – but the staff? It would surely give her away, and she could not discard it. It was her biggest problem, unless she somehow hid *it* in plain sight. Suddenly, she grinned to herself. It was a grim smile, tinged with memories of Lanrik, for thinking of him had given her the answers she needed and a definite course of action.

She got up, left the sweetshop, and strode once more down the Hainer Lon. Only now, she had a destination in mind.

She walked carefully, with her eyes wide open and her senses alert. Three times she saw guards, and three times she managed to put the crowd in the street between her and them, and hide the staff on the far side of her body. She was breathless from anxiety by the time she reached her destination.

She stepped into the shop. It was a place oppose the Hamalath, one of several where actors and dramatists bought clothes and equipment for performances in the open-air theatre.

She took an empty wicker basket from near the serving counter and wandered around, looking through the bundles of clothes and different materials. She pulled things out as she found what she was after, and then she went to the far corner where the makeup supplies were kept. She took what she needed from there and placed those items in the basket with the rest. After a final look around, she went back to the counter.

A young boy stood behind it, ready to serve, though he seemed disinterested in the whole process. He looked over her items, told her how much it all came to, and she paid. She did not have the time to haggle, and the goods were already cheap. Most actors were not well paid.

"Can I change in here?" she asked.

114

The boy obviously thought it a strange request, but he waved her toward a little room out the back.

"In there," he said abruptly.

She went inside and put her new clothes on. It took her some time until she was satisfied. On the way out, she left the basket at the counter and gave the boy a goodbye wave. He ignored her, and she wondered what his problem was. But rude serving boys were all over the city. When she found a shop with friendly staff, she always went back. It did not matter that it was all fake, all part of the process of selling her things. She understood that, but all that mattered was that she had a good time. But despite the serving boy, this shop still gave her a smile.

She stepped onto the street, but no longer looked like Erlissa. Or Tamril. The makeup was of a dull gray tone, and it made the skin of her face and hands look old. And she wore a wig, a thing of real hair, long and gray and straggly. Her outer clothes, worn over the top of a new dress, were raggedy. Best of all, they were padded underneath with wool in all the right places to make her look fat. And a good job they did of it, too. She wondered if she would look like that in truth one day. If she kept eating seed cakes, she would.

She pursed her lips a few times, working her mouth because it felt uncomfortable. It was dry, for there were balls of wool pressed into the sides of her cheeks. They made her face look fatter.

Now, she looked like an old lady who actually needed a staff to help her walk. She hobbled down the street, and looked carefully about her. Nobody paid her any attention. None at all. She might as well have been invisible. She was not used to that, but today, it suited her. She smiled, aware that brown dye stained her teeth and made them look bad. That made her chuckle, and

115

she changed her voice as she did so into a semblance of a wheezy cackle.

Then she thought of Lanrik, and the smile fell from her haggard face. To all the world she was a bitter old lady, and in truth, that was how she felt.

12. Into the Light

The charred-man twitched and shrugged.

Lanrik watched it. For a moment, nothing else in the world mattered. The creature would either dive into the water, or it would not. He would either live, or he would die.

From afar, he heard the sounds of bird calls in the park. The real world, the world of light and love and laughter, was within reach. But here, in this closed off and muted twilight, it was possible to believe that those things were only dreams. The charred-man was the one reality that counted, and the malice of Ebona that sustained and drove him.

Lanrik treaded water. His sword was heavy in its sheath, and his boots weighed him down. He should act. He should continue to flee this thing, but at the same time, he had to watch and find out what it would do. Had hope cheated him, faint though it was?

With a body-shuddering shrug and a spasm of frenzied twitching, the charred-man opened his mouth and screamed. Or scream it would have been if he voiced a sound. But though his head lifted, and his neck extended like a wolf howling his misery to the world, no sound broke the primordial stillness of the aqueduct. Instead, fire and smoke clouded the air before him as though he was a man whose breath turned into a mist-cloud on a cold morning.

The charred-man suddenly turned and lurched away, unable to force himself to dare the waters, no matter that the sorcery of Ebona drove him. That it pained him was obvious, and even in the midst of relief, Lanrik spared a thought for the man the thing had once been.

For a moment, he closed his eyes. But he knew the charred-man had not given up. Nor had the guards. He must take the next step to get out of here, and disappear from those who sought him.

It seemed doubtful that the charred-man still had the power of speech, though there were other means of communication. Either way, he must assume that in time his pursuer would alert the guards of where he was last seen. Therefore, he must get out of the aqueduct swiftly.

He hoped Erlissa had been as lucky as he had. For though the creature had pursued him, the streets were not safe. They never had been from the very start of this quest, but they had only grown worse. The only thing he could do now was to get into the Haranast and hope to find her there.

The bright light from above drew his attention. There were several openings, some grated, others uncovered. No doubt at times of drought they would all be in use. At the moment, he saw no movement from above, and no activity of gardeners; but they would be there, or nearby. Still, it was the way out, for large buckets held by long ropes hung down and provided the escape he was looking for.

None of the buckets rested in the water. Most were visible, hanging just below the opening in the dome above, and a few were in various stages of suspension between.

He struck out toward the lowest one. The splashing was loud in his ears, for it echoed hollowly from the stone-vaulted ceiling.

Reaching for the bucket, he found that it was too high. He treaded water, positioned himself better, and pushed up again as best he could. His hand caught the wooden side of the pail, but he could not get a proper grip and sank down once more beneath the water.

He came to the surface, more grateful than ever that his ploy with the charred-man had worked. For if the creature could swim, he would have been unable to continue fleeing from it. Yet he was still trapped, whether pursued or not, and he had to reason his way through the problem and come up with a solution.

After a few moments, an idea occurred to him and he took off his sword and belt. He tied the end of the belt to the hardened leather sheath. He held the naked blade with one hand, and with the other threw his improvised rope over the bucket.

Several times he failed, but he got better after a few attempts, and at length he managed to spear the sheath through the gap between handle and bucket.

Having done that, he brought the two ends of his improvised rope together and hauled himself up.

The bucket swung ponderously from side to side, but the rope fixed to its metal handle held. The buckets were quite large, and they were designed to haul up heavy loads of water. Somewhere above the end of the rope was fixed to a secure post in the ground, and he hoped that it did not move up there. Otherwise, a gardener might come to investigate.

He managed to stand with his feet on the bucket and one hand gripping the rope. With the other, he re-sheathed the blade and then threaded the belt back into the loops of his pants. It was a difficult job while holding onto a swaying rope, but he persisted until it was done. He could not climb until both hands were free.

When he was finished, he rested a moment. The rope stopped swinging so much, and he caught his breath. Climbing would not be easy, but he soon set to it, using his feet to hook the rope and provide some purchase, while he heaved himself up by his arms.

He rested several times, for the effort was great. His arms ached, and his legs began to cramp. But he could not afford to stop for long.

At length, he neared the opening. His eyes adjusted to the ever-brighter light, but he could see nothing except blue sky. It was the faded blue of late afternoon. The day had been very long and sudden weariness overtook him. But he knew that if he rested too long now, he would only cool down and stiffen up. He must keep moving.

It was too late to reach the Haranast today. Tomorrow, he would meet up with Erlissa, for the races started early each morning and ran at intervals until midafternoon.

With a final heave he lifted himself until his head cleared the opening, and he looked about him.

He was in the middle of the park. It was usually just called *the* park, though some people referred to it as Conhain's Rest. It was a strange name for a place that the king had never been to, for the city was only built after his death, although some people said that his bones were reburied here years after the battle in which he had died. At any rate, there was a monument to him not that far away.

All about him he saw bright gardens and green grass. Nearby was some shrubbery, no doubt to hide the wells from those who enjoyed the park. But strangely, he saw no people. During the day there should have been scores, even hundreds wandering around or lying down. And yet it was eerily silent. He could not understand it.

He waited and watched. Soon, the answer was evident. There *were* people. They rimmed the entire perimeter of the park, many hundreds of paces away in every direction that he could see. But they were not civilians. He saw them move from time to time, saw the color of their uniforms, and the telltale jut of sword sheaths by their side. They were soldiers. Soldiers, and a scattering of Royal Guards. How could they have found him so quickly?

He watched some more, cursing under his breath. And yet they made no move to enter the park. They stayed just where they were, like a line of sentries, and did not advance toward him or conduct any kind of search.

Were they even here for him? The longer he watched, the more he doubted it, and yet why were they here at all, if *not* for him? They looked as if they were guarding something, but there was nothing of value here.

It was time to move. This was no place to be caught if a gardener, or anybody else, came along. He put the mystery of the soldiers to the back of his mind, and eased out of the well. The stone rim was smooth, worn from years of ropes rubbing along its surface, and he slipped out of it slowly, like a snake from a hole. He watched for any sign of movement about him, careful that his own movements were slow and steady so as not to attract attention.

He stayed low to the ground, using the Raithlin Crawl to move to the nearest shrubbery. Once there, he paused. For now, he was out of sight, but not out of danger. He had escaped the charred-man and the aqueduct. The park must be next, and yet he could not risk an attempt during daylight. There were too many eyes nearby, even for a Raithlin.

He moved though the bushes, seeking higher ground. There was none, but one shrub was taller than the others, reaching up ten feet or so and thick with dark foliage. He climbed it, careful of his weight on the small branches, and looked out.

There were no gardeners anywhere. None at all. And he saw that plants within many rows of flowerbeds had wilted. They had not been watered for some time.

It was all passing strange, a thing beyond his understanding, and he could see no reason for it. But the Witch-queen did nothing by accident, and a reason for the presence of the soldiers, a very good one, must exist.

The westering rays of the sun glared brightly now, a final fare of light at just the right angle to blind him, but soon it would set, and he would be on the move again. For the moment, he rested, secure in his hiding spot, and drying out. His leather boots would become stiff and uncomfortable, but that was of little matter. Running would not serve him now, only the skills of the Raithlin, for he would need to treat his next movements as though he was a scout in the wilderness, and his own countrymen an enemy army.

Dark shadows marched across the park. The first star twinkled high above. It was faint, but the sky deepened like a slowly shuttered lamp, and soon many more sprang into view.

He slipped down from his hiding spot and moved across the grass. He no longer crawled, but walked, seeking out and using all the low points in the ground, stalking between hedges and flowerbeds like a creature of the night that shunned men.

He moved toward the Hainer Lon. It was a better place to hide in the evening than it was during the day. And he no longer carried the staff. At night, he could get by without being overly worried of being caught, at least until the streets went quiet.

It was not the first time that he had to try to slip through a line of sentries. Even so, this would be difficult. The soldiers had been placed at twenty feet intervals. Ebona was taking no chances that anything would get into the park. Or, he supposed, get out of it. Although what would get in, or out, was still a mystery too deep to fathom.

He drew nearer to the Hainer Lon, and the sentries who lined it. It might be dark now, but the moon would rise later and bathe the park in silvery light. He must be gone before that happened.

A grove of oaks, ancient and gnarly, angled between him and his destination. It would make good cover if he passed through it, but it was also a place of fallen leaves and branches, the sort of environment where it would be harder to avoid making noises that alerted the guards. Better to move alongside it, than within it. Besides, he did not know what lurked within. The guards watched for *something*.

As he passed he heard the rattle of voles in dead leaves, and the hoot of owls. Small insects chirped, and large beetles clicked their wings in the dark. Mosquitoes swarmed. One, more persistent than the others, whined near his face, but he ignored it as best he could. He stalked ahead silently and slowly, until suddenly he froze in place. Something moved in the shadows of the grove.

A moment later it paced out in front of him, unaware of his presence. It was a fox. When it saw him, it too stood still. They both stared at each other, each as surprised as the other. But then it trotted away, not alarmed or scared, but surefooted and definite in its desire to remove itself from the area. Lanrik smiled. The fox and he were brothers tonight.

He moved ahead. The grove dwindled to a few large trees, and then there was nothing between him and the Hainer Lon but a hundred or so paces of lawn. And the sentries. He could see their silhouettes by the light of the city behind them.

It was time for the Raithlin Crawl again, and he slipped down to his hands and knees and then his belly. He moved ahead, palms on the earth, elbows close to his body to provide support and eliminate any chance of being silhouetted himself. His weight rested on his forearms and one leg at a time, and he lifted his body just enough to avoid making scraping sounds as he progressed.

The grass was short and provided no cover, but at least it was green and not a source of potential noise. He crept onward, aware that from this point he might be visible if he moved too fast or rose too high off the ground. He took care that each of his movements was only the minimum needed, and that they were carried out with patience.

The minutes passed. The stars twinkled ever more brightly. He breathed slowly, moved slowly, and sought out even the slightest depression in the ground that might help him.

He had an advantage. The sentries stood, and they would be looking out beyond him into the park. He knew they were there, but they did not know of his presence. They would not think anything could be so close, and the focus of their attention would be out and beyond him.

He kept his head down, for the shine of his pale face in the faint light of the city would certainly give him away. From time to time, he rested. He could not see the sentries, but he listened. He heard no talking, or steps, or any warning that something was amiss. Noise from the buildings and streets had grown louder as he approached, and that would help him should he accidentally make any noise of his own.

The sound of a horse-drawn carriage rolled down the Hainer Lon. The wheels clattered against the stone cobbles and the horse's hooves clopped loudly. Whoever it was must be someone important, for carriages were seldom seen on the main thoroughfare of Esgallien. It was a place of shops and markets, and the people did not like being disturbed when other roads would serve the driver just as well. But Lanrik did not mind. Not tonight, for it would redirect the guards' attention from the park to the road behind them.

The noise swelled. He waited until it was near its peak, and then moved ahead faster. He lifted his head as the carriage drew near level with him. Sure enough, he could clearly see the two nearest soldiers and they had both turned to watch the carriage.

Lanrik took a deep breath. What he was about to do was risky, but he still had a chance to run if things went badly. If they went well though, he was through.

He stood up and strode ahead until he was nearly level with the sentries. It took only a few moments. The carriage rattled past, and he put the rest of his plan into action.

"Eyes to the front, soldiers!" he barked.

The men snapped around and looked at him. It was too dark to see him properly, and he hoped they could not tell that he was not in a uniform. The order should be enough for them to assume he was a captain.

"Yes, Sir!" said one.

"Sorry, Sir!" said the other.

"Save your apologies for the Witch-queen," he answered.

Even in the dark he felt a wave of fear from them. They were soldiers, not Royal Guards, and he did not think they had any love for her. It was better to slip through this way, if he could, than be forced to harm one of them to make a gap in the line.

They gave no further answer, and he strode ahead, keeping to his guise. But when he passed out of their sight and into the view of others, he changed his stride from the stiff and upright pacing of a soldier to the staggering walk of a reveling citizen.

Now, he was on the very edge of the Hainer Lon, and there were pedestrians not too far away. He wanted to be taken as one of them. The soldiers ignored him, and with a few more steps he had cobbles under his feet and was drifting away from the park with a sense of relief.

He let out a long breath and turned his mind to what was next. He knew this much: he could not spend the night at an inn. They would be watched. And though there were many of them, and they could not *all* be watched, he could not know which ones were safe and which ones were not.

Nor could he seek the help of anyone that he knew; even those with whom he had only had a passing association. They might be watched as well. He thought about it as he walked along the Hainer Lon, and soon realized that he could not stay here much longer, either. Even though it was still early in the evening, the streets were far less crowded than during the day. And it would soon grow much quieter. The guards would be sure to patrol it, and an isolated pedestrian had nowhere to hide.

It did not take him too long to reach a decision as to what he must do. Even in that little time, the streets became quieter. It seemed as though night in Esgallien was even more dangerous than the day, and people stayed at home, behind bolted doors.

Clouds started to roll in from the east, and their dark masses swallowed the stars. A chill wind picked up, carrying the scent of distant rain, and he knew it was going to be a long and miserable night.

He passed a narrow side street, and there he paused. A good while he looked down it, but the sudden noise of tramping boots somewhere ahead on the Hainer Lon forced his final decision. It might only be late night revelers, but it might also be guards. Either could be dangerous.

He stepped down the street. Here, he drew his sword. It was dark, for little light from lanterns spilled out of the tenement buildings. It was the sort of place where thieves and brigands lurked, waiting for their prey.

A tall building rose to the left, and he glided toward it. The shadows were deeper here, and that would better hide him. More than that, if he was attacked, the wall would stop a group from being able to surrounding him.

He stopped and listened, but heard nothing. The breeze blew icy-cold down the tunnel formed by the buildings. He heard the pitter-patter of rain on roofs, and then the first drops sprinkled his skin.

The shower did not last. By the time it had finished he was further down the street, creeping with all the skills he had learned in the wilderness as a Raithlin, for surely the city was a wild place in its own way. And the Raithlin principles of concealment did not change, no matter the surroundings: the eye recognized movement first, silhouette second and color last. So he moved slowly, kept close to the wall to ensure he was not outlined against either end of the street, and stayed in the shadows.

He came to a corner. It was, as he hoped, an alley. This was even more dangerous, and though thieves were common enough, they could not prowl every pool of shadow.

The sword felt light in his hand, and for the first time he raised it, but did not extend it too far in front of him.

That would only make it easy for someone to knock it to the side.

When he went around the turn, he stepped wide from the wall for the first time. Spotting a potential threat around the corner was more important than remaining unseen.

The alley was a river of blackness, and the rough cobbles under his boots were slippery with moisture. But he saw nothing except a cat. It looked at him for a moment to see what he would do, and then it slinked away in the opposite direction. It did not come back, so likely enough, no one else was there.

He moved back into the deeper shadows near the wall. In the distance, he heard singing and raucous laughter, and further away the barking of several dogs. Satisfied that he was all alone, he studied the building close to him until he found what he wanted. It was only two stories high, short for the city, and it was a near windowless place that lacked any cheer. What it did have was a front door: a sturdy construction that was closed, and no doubt bolted. It also had a drainpipe of oven-hardened clay, and this was what interested him.

He ran his hands along the surface of the pipe. It was slick with moisture, and cold, but seemed strong enough for what he intended to do.

With a final look around him to reassure himself that no one was watching, he sheathed his sword. He put hands and feet to the pipe and climbed. It was slow and difficult going, but he reached the second floor soon enough. The pipe ended here, coming out from the wall of what was likely a bathroom. He was not done climbing, though. He peered through a narrow window, grated by iron bars. No one was visible inside, and no lantern was lit, either. He climbed some more until he could stand up on the sill, and reached above him until his hands had as good a grip as he could get on the edge of the tiled roof.

With a sudden heave he drew himself up. The slick tiles were dangerous, and he nearly lost his grip, but he pulled and twisted until he slid up over the edge of the roof. It had been more dangerous than he thought it would be, and he was no good with heights. Had he known, he would have thought of something else. And yet he was here now. It was a safe place, for no one could find him here, and though there were taller buildings nearby, their lights were mostly out, indicating that those who lived there had gone to bed.

He moved high up the roof, careful not to make any noise, and careful not to go so far as to be silhouetted on the skyline. The view would have been better if he went all the way, but likewise, he would be more easily spotted.

He lied down on his back and studied what was visible of the city. He could see many streets, and the odd group of revelers. He closed his eyes and slept, but not for long. A cold shower woke him. His face dripped water and the tiles were cold beneath his wet clothes. He turned to his side and then grew still.

From a street nearby he heard the drum of marching feet, and then a group of Royal Guards came into view. For a moment he saw them turn into the Hainer Lon, their uniforms lit by a lantern hanging at the front of an inn, and then they were gone.

A while later he saw the charred-man. The strange creature wandered down a dark street to the left, oblivious that the prey it so desperately sought was watching it. Lanrik could not mistake its twitching and lurching gait. He would never forget that so long as he lived.

For a brief moment the flickering eyes turned in his direction, and his blood froze, but then the creature was gone, disappearing down another street.

The night was cold and miserable. Sleep was a fleeting thing that came and went, never staying long. It was still dark when a cockcrow signaled the approaching dawn.

Lanrik sat up, rubbed his eyes and summoned his courage. He would need it today, for at the break of light he would slip away from his hiding place and seek out the Haranast. Getting there might not be a problem; it was not that far away. Finding Erlissa was what worried him.

What if she did not come?

13. Swords, Curses and Confusion

Dawn was newly born when Lanrik made a start of getting down from the roof.

If he had left it too late, and people walked into the alley, he would be taken as a thief. But if he had moved sooner, he would have been at risk of running into a patrol of guards on the streets, with nobody else there to distract their attention.

He hoped that he had judged it just right.

One thing that he was not counting on was the danger of being seen from within the tenement building. He had heard no noises, and assumed none of the occupants were up yet, but he was mistaken.

Just as he started to move down the drainpipe, he looked through the grated window. A middle-aged woman was there, half naked, watching him. One moment their eyes met. One moment they both remained still, and then she screamed. The sound was so high pitched, so shrill, that he feared it would carry for a half-mile in every direction and bring the entire city down on his back.

He turned bright red, realizing that he had been taken for something worse than a thief, for surely no woman ever cried out like that for fear of burglary – not when an iron-grated window barred the way.

He half climbed, half fell down the rest of the pipe. His feet were moving before they even touched the rough cobbles, and then he was racing down the alley. He went back the way he had come last night, not knowing what was down the other end.

A door slammed, there were shouts somewhere behind him, and then with a rush he turned a corner into the Hainer Lon.

He should have risked the other end of the alley, even though he did not know what was there. For what he saw now turned his face from red to white. Two Royal Guards stood just ahead of him, looking at him strangely. In his haste, he had run straight at them.

He did not hesitate. In one quick motion he used all his forward momentum and rammed his left elbow into the face of the nearest one. There was a dull thud. The man collapsed, unconscious, and blood streamed from his nose onto his chest.

Without pause, Lanrik moved onto the other guard. The man attempted to draw his sword, but Lanrik was quicker. He struck out with his right fist. The smack of the sudden blow resounded like a whip-crack on the Hainer Lon.

He followed up with three more punches, fast and well placed. Then he was off again, racing away even as the man fell to the ground.

It was not a good start to the day. And yet, in its way, luck had favored him. There had only been two guards, and he had disabled them. They could not chase him. Or if they did, his lead would be too great for them to do any good by the time they managed to get up.

He turned down a side street and sprinted as fast as he could. There were people here, but not many, and no one interfered.

Zigzagging through a succession of streets, he came to a sudden stop. There was nobody behind him. He had not heard any sort of alarm – the guards might be unconscious – and to keep on running now would only draw attention to himself. It was time to walk.

Inadvertently, he had gone in the wrong direction. Before running into the guards, he had meant to head toward the city's center and go straight to the Haranast. But he had been disoriented in his mad dash and now must be somewhere near the park from which he had escaped yesterday.

As his breath came back, he grew hungry. Soon, it felt as though hollowness gnawed away at his insides. He decided to do two things at once.

The Hainer Lon was close. He still stayed off it, but followed a parallel course until he was level with where he thought the middle of the park would be. At that point, he carefully made his way back.

There were more people on the Hainer Lon now, although it was not busy yet. He walked along it swiftly until he found what he was after.

He approached a baker's shop and ordered a loaf. Casually glancing around while the bread was retrieved from the back, he studied the guards. The picket line remained in place, and it watched and waited for something, though what it was, he still could not guess. And yet it must be vital to expend so much manpower on it. They had been there for at least a day, and that was just what he knew of.

He gave the baker some coins and jerked his thumb back at the guards.

"How long have they been there?"

The baker, a jovial man with red hair and an easy smile, looked suddenly wary, but he answered after a pause.

"Two weeks," he said slowly. "Maybe more. And my sales went down from day one."

Lanrik understood. No one wanted to go near soldiers in Esgallien. Not since the Witch-queen controlled them.

133

He thanked the man and headed down a side street. He had seen and heard enough.

He ate the loaf as he walked. It was still hot inside, and truly, he thought, there was nothing better than freshly baked bread. All it needed was butter. Then again, hunger was the keenest inducement to flavor. Either way, he ate it with enormous relish.

He moved along the side streets, and the city grew increasingly busy. He saw no more guards, or soldiers, but knew they were about. There was still no alarm, and he wondered if the guards that he had attacked even knew it was him that had done it. It could, he supposed, have been taken as a random attack from a criminal escaping the location of his crime. That would especially be the case if someone from the tenement building came out onto the street to chase him.

The Hainer Lon was always close; all streets in Esgallien led to it, or from it, and when he was ready he maneuvered his way back. But he did not intend to follow it for any great length.

The Haranast was very close, and he arrived there after only a few moments.

An extended series of granite arches opened before him. Nearby was a basalt stele dedicated to Conmur, the king's grandfather, who had ordered the facility's construction at vast cost and with great labor.

He passed through the ancient granite arches and was instantly met by a low hum of noise from the people already gathered there, although no race had yet been run. The Haranast accommodated ten thousand people, and though there were perhaps only a thousand here now, it seemed near empty. He picked his way down several long aisles of the terraced hillside, heading toward the stables where he had asked Erlissa to meet him.

Far below was the track. Sand covered all of its one hundred and fifty paces. Competitors would ride its length, taking multiple and dangerous turns around carved posts at each end.

One post served as a starting point, and the other as a finish line. He headed toward the finish, where the stables were also located, and wondered if Erlissa was already there.

He could not see her, for it was still too far away, and the largest portion of the crowd was milling about there. The finish line was the most popular place to watch from.

A horn blew three long notes. A race was soon to begin, and his gaze wandered to the stable entrances at the base of the hill.

Somewhere below ground were not just stables, but also rooms for the riders, the trainers and all of the Haranast staff. It was strange to think of all those spaces and people below ground, but he had heard that there was a maze of tunnels down there, hidden from the spectators.

Some wooden gates swung open at one of the entrances. He continued to angle his way toward the finish line, watching as a half dozen horses trotted out. There was an enthusiastic cheer from the crowd.

Some of the riders urged their mounts into a light gallop to warm up their muscles; others waved to the crowd and merely walked their horses up to the starting post. Perhaps there was sufficient space below ground to actually run the horses without needing to come out onto the track.

The horses were all fine animals. They were sleek, well muscled and kept at the peak of health and fitness. At least, that's what the trainers always told anyone who ever asked about them. The owners sometimes had a different point of view.

He wondered for the first time how his own horse, the alar stallion that he had taken from the shazrahad, would fare in these races. That it had endurance beyond Esgallien's horses, he did not doubt. It could keep on galloping long after anything here had lost its wind. But could it match them for speed?

The riders drew their horses level with the starting post, and the crowd grew excited. He was still some way from the finish line. But he was much lower in the stadium now, and row after row of stone benches rose above him on the terraced hill. The arched exits seemed far away.

Some said there were also exits from the underground rooms, used by the riders and Haranast staff. He had never seen them. It was always a problem for people to get in and out of here, the arches being so few and the crowds so large. That was probably why so many races were run each day of the week and right from morning until midafternoon. It spread things out instead of concentrating them at peak times.

Some of the crowd's excitement washed off on him as he watched the beginning of the race. The horses sped along, sand spraying behind them, brave riders bent low over their backs. It was a dangerous sport, and many was the people's favorite whose career had ended in a fall. Sadly, the same sometimes applied to horses. But the races were safer than they were in Esgallien's past. In the early days of settlement, riders often fought with wooden swords as they raced. That had not occurred for many hundreds of years, although under the Witch-queen, anything, no matter how cruel, might be reintroduced. Especially if it provided entertainment and shifted the attention of the people away from what really mattered.

136

The lead rider reached the finish post, but the race was far from over. He turned, and sand churned up from flying hooves to thicken the air. A second later, the others followed in a large pack after him. They galloped back the other way, for the race still had several laps to go.

He was close to the finish post now. He took his gaze from the track and looked for Erlissa. He did not see her. But there were many people here. Some were robed, and some cloaked, and many of the spectators were women. But he saw no sign of the girl he most wanted to see.

He moved as close to the finish post as he could, and stood with the others nearby to watch the rest of the race.

The contest was coming to its last lap. The lead rider had gained a few more lengths on the rest. He still bent low, but now his whip was out and he urged the horse on. Sweat coated its flanks. Its nostrils flared to take in more air. The riders behind shouted and brought down their whips rapidly.

From out of the midst of the pack a white-socked sorrel emerged. It outpaced the others and gained ground on the leader. The crowd roared.

This rider did not use his whip so much. He was a very slight man, the smallest there, perhaps no more than a boy. But Lanrik recognized the skill shown by his easy balance and the way his weight and motions were one with the great horse beneath him.

The sorrel surged ahead of the pack and drew near to the lead horse. In a few more strides, they were neck and neck. The other rider whipped furiously, but his mount was tiring and had nothing left to give. The sorrel stayed with it a moment longer, and then with a final burst of speed, strained ahead to win by nearly a length.

The crowd roared. Men yelled and women clapped. Lanrik stood where he was. He looked for Erlissa, subdued in the midst of all the excitement.

He sat down when the clamor subsided, and the majority of people had also taken their seats. He was less visible this way, but he did not want to stand out from the crowd. Anyway, if Erlissa came here, she would see him. He felt suddenly sick. What if she did not come? What if he never saw her again?

There was usually a good while between races. It gave the spectators time to talk and drink. He did neither, but watched idly as boys came out onto the track with large rakes and leveled the churned-up sand.

The horses stayed at one end of the arena, walking and moving to cool down. There they remained for some while until the riders got down and handlers took the reins.

A few minutes later the stable doors opened again and the horses were led underground. There must be lights there too, many of them, otherwise the horses would balk. It must in fact be huge down there, open and well lit. Lanrik realized that no matter how well he knew Esgallien, there was always more to learn. The city was a fabulous place, ancient and mysterious even to its inhabitants.

It was also a place of fear, at least nowadays. And that was abruptly brought home to him. The crowd went suddenly quiet. He did not know why at first, but after looking around for a few moments he saw that a dozen Royal Guards had entered the Haranast. They were far away, but the cringe of the people near them gave them away as much as their uniforms.

Lanrik watched them carefully. That they were looking for someone was obvious. They moved along the aisles, checking faces as they went. They could not go through each aisle though, and they might or might not come to his. It was a roll of the dice. And if he tried to leave now, it would only attract the attention that he was desperate to avoid.

He remained where he was, and watched and waited. The guards stuck together. Although they could cover more ground by splitting up, they worked as a group, staying in close proximity to each other at all times.

It signaled to him that they were scared of the crowd, or, he supposed, scared of him, for he was the one that they were most likely looking for.

A grim smile came to his lips. If they were scared of him, it was because he had taught them to be so. But even so, there were too many of them to fight. And he could not count on any help from the crowd. Although he could not discount it either. They had helped yesterday.

The people of Esgallien might be cowed, but the spark of defiance was not gone. He did not want to inflame it. Not here, not now. The guards had swords and unarmed people would die. He did not want that.

The guards came closer. He no longer watched, but kept his eyes on the track. They were near enough now that they might recognize him. He sat in a casual posture, one leg crossed over the other. It helped hide the sword sheathed at his side.

The crowd grew still about him. And deadly silent. They knew this was a moment of potential danger, if not the reason why. Rumor of a Raithlin on the loose would have spread since yesterday.

He waited, using the crowd's reaction to judge where the guards were. They had come very close.

A shadow fell upon him. The first guard neared. The man looked down at him, and Lanrik suppressed the urge to run. Instead, he looked up, allowing a slightly annoyed expression to show on his face. He had no choice but to look. Although it made him easier to recognize, not to do so was unnatural in the circumstances and would indicate that he wanted to hide. There was always the chance that the guard had never seen him in person and that his grasp of a verbal description would not be enough.

The guard paused. He looked to go on, but then he hesitated and shifted his gaze back.

For a few moments he stared hard, and then in sudden recognition staggered back to get out of Lanrik's way. The man drew his sword. Fear was on his face, but in a moment it hardened as his comrades rushed to stand beside him.

The game was over. All of the guards were near. Lanrik drew his own sword.

He held the blade high, and it glinted in the light. Once more he heard whispers as its famous etching glinted and shimmered in the sun.

Raithlin. The crowd murmured it, the word passing from lip to ear and then to lip again. They backed away from him, but they did not run.

All of a sudden, he felt like he was in a sword tournament. A crowd watched. And he had an opposition. Only there were many of them and but one of him. He stepped forward anyway.

At the same time, an old lady trudged past Lanrik and approached the group. She held a walking staff in her tremulous hands. Her skin was leathered by hard work and blotched with age.

"Go back, lady," Lanrik said. "This is no place for you. Move away to safety."

The old lady tilted her head and looked at him.

"What a well-mannered boy you are," she said wheezily. "A pity that these Royal Guards aren't more like you."

She turned to them and poked at the nearest with her staff.

"Stand aside!" she ordered. "I'm too old to go around. And anyway, why should I?"

"I don't care what you do, old lady," the guard said. "Stay or go. Live or die. It's all the same to us. But we're taking this man to the queen, and she won't care anymore than we do if you get killed during the process."

The old lady trembled and coughed. Her hands looked like ancient parchment, and yet their grip upon the staff was firm. Lanrik looked more closely at the timber. It was walnut. It was covered in dust. Mud caked either end. But he suddenly knew it.

He stood perfectly still. The whole world seemed to pause. And then he spoke.

"The Witch-queen may not care if this lady dies. But I do. I care very much."

He raised his sword and stepped forward.

"Drop your weapon!" One of the guards said. "Come with us peacefully!"

"Or die," another added.

Lanrik laughed. He felt something inside him break free, something that he always held on a tight leash.

"No," he said. "I'll kill you all before I go to the Witch-queen."

He stepped forward another pace. His every movement suggested defiance. They read it in his eyes. And yet he made no move, nor did blade touch blade before the battle began.

The old lady, or Erlissa, for he now knew who she was, brought down the end of her staff against the stone paving. Caked mud sprayed everywhere. A great boom thundered through the Haranast. Blue flame turned and twisted, running across the stone before leaping high into the air.

The guards cursed and reeled back. The crowd screamed and fled. All was confusion, and people were everywhere, running and stumbling.

Lanrik, with Erlissa right next to him, jumped down to the next row of seats. Together they moved down several more rows. People fled from them toward the guards. People fled from the guards *toward* them. In the mass of movement, they ran along a suddenly empty aisle and toward the arched exits. But escape was far away, and the guards close, even if they were momentarily hidden by the turmoil.

14. Wrath of the Witch-queen

Lanrik and Erlissa raced ahead. The path between seats was wide, and they moved swiftly, catching up to those who had fled before them.

Abruptly, a wall of people blocked their path. And yet there was a wall behind them too, pressing forward. The guards were somewhere within it, though Lanrik could not see them.

Progress was now very slow. Higher up, at the crest of the hill, many people streamed out to safety beneath the arches. And yet where Lanrik was now, the crowd only shuffled, one desperate step at a time.

Those who had seen them earlier were elsewhere now, swept away in the wild surge of the crowd. No one recognized Lanrik or Erlissa, or knew that they had been at the center of the disturbance, nor that he was a Raithlin and she a lòhren. They were just two more people struggling to flee. The crowd seethed. It pushed and shoved, sped up and slowed down. But they stayed together.

"Over that way," Lanrik said.

He took Erlissa's hand, and they changed direction slightly. They could not get ahead any faster, but they were able to drift sideways, a little at a time. He wanted to ensure that the guards did not find them. They would have seen the direction that he and Erlissa had originally taken, and that was where they would follow.

Lanrik heard a lot of yelling and curses, but no screams. It seemed as though the guards were not using their swords to force their way through. That choice was probably a matter of self-preservation more than anything else. In such a crowded space, where people had nowhere to go to escape, necessity would compel them to fight back. And though they were mostly unarmed, and it would be muscle against steel, the mass of their numbers would prevail in the end. And the guards knew it.

He kept a tight hold of Erlissa's hand. He did not think he would ever let go of it again. It felt so good to be with her once more. And suddenly, hope filled him. The Lindrath was still alive. They would find him, and surely none knew better than he how things stood in the city, and what the queen's weaknesses were, and which of her enemies were willing to fight. They would escape with him and meet with Aranloth as arranged. After that, the end of the Witch-queen's reign would come swiftly. Of that, he was sure.

A gap opened in the crowd before them as a line of people further ahead surged through the exits. They moved into it.

"I still don't see any guards," Erlissa said.

"They're there somewhere," he answered. "We've been lucky so far."

The crowd started to move even more quickly. The arches were close now, and people were streaming through them. They started to run again.

In moments, they stood beneath the shadow of one of the great archways themselves, near to the stele that commemorated the building of the Haranast.

"Where to?" Erlissa asked.

Lanrik looked down the Hainer Lon to the right. A troop of guards was coming up that way against the rush of the crowd. He looked to the left, and saw the same. The Royal Guard were converging here to see what had caused the disturbance. He felt trapped yet again, for though there were many people here, the chances of slipping through unnoticed, with so many watchful eyes about, was slim.

He glanced at Erlissa. "We might have to run for it. Either way, it'll probably turn into a fight." He squeezed her hand. "Be careful."

A moment she looked at him, as though undecided about something, and then her face set hard with determination.

"There's another way," she said.

He watched silently as she took off her wig, cast it aside, and removed the outer layer of her clothes. They were raggedy and filled with some kind of stuffing that made her look bigger. Underneath, what she wore amazed him.

It was as though the Witch-queen herself stood before him. Erlissa, tall and athletic, always of a likeness to Ebona in build, now wore the same white dress, cinched by a red belt. Her hair, dyed blonde by Aranloth before they entered the city, completed the effect.

She now looked so similar to their enemy that his heart fluttered in his chest. The disguise was uncannily accurate, and it scared him. It might also scare others, which was a two-sided situation. She might fool the guards, but at the same time it was a way to get killed, for the crowd, who surely hated their newest ruler, might turn on her.

But she showed no hesitation.

"Take this," she ordered, handing him her staff. "Stay behind me."

He did not argue. It was as though she had adopted not only the likeness of the Witch-queen, but her commanding presence also. She strode ahead, straight toward the group of guards coming from the right.

145

When they were close, she raised a long arm and pointed at them.

"Fools!" she said. Her eyes flashed, and her voice dripped venom. She lowered her hand, but as she did so red drops of flame dribbled from the fingertips. She shuddered, as though battling some inner desire to wreak havoc and unleash her temper upon the world.

The crowd screamed and ran. But the guards, held by duty, faced her, though their expressions showed fear. Lanrik did not blame them.

"Fools!" she repeated. "This is a diversion. Our enemies seek to free the prisoners at the palace."

One of the men stepped forward. He did not look at her, but kept his gaze to the ground as he spoke.

"But aren't all the prisoners dead?" he queried.

Erlissa tilted her head, and her blonde hair swung in front of her eyes. She ran her hand through it, placing it behind her ear, and stared at the man until he eventually looked up.

"Do you know all my secrets?" she asked in a soft voice.

The man dropped his head again, and his shoulders trembled. "No, My Lady."

"No. You do not. There are yet prisoners alive. The most important of them all. And while you tremble before me like a cowering dog, they might even now be escaping."

Erlissa paused. Sparks kindled in her eyes, and a dark shadow fell from her tall figure. She lifted her arm again. Red fire flared to life on her palm, like a ball of light that writhed and twisted, straining to break away into a stream that would burn all in its path.

"Hasten!" she commanded. "Go to the palace. There are Raithlin there. Kill them. Kill them all – or die yourselves!"

146

She pulled back her arm as though to fling the witch-fire, but she need not have bothered. No one saw this final threat. The guards were already sprinting toward the palace, fear driving them faster than duty ever could.

Lanrik was amazed. Erlissa looked at him, and her eyes were still ablaze. She seemed queen of the world, her face filled with power and authority. She was remote, like a beautiful figure of carved ice, but without passion or thought or heart. Only power. And then she winked at him. The slight movement seemed so strange on that face, so bizarre, that he laughed.

She flashed him a smile in return, and Ebona was gone. She was Erlissa again. She undid the red belt, and tucked it within a fold of her white dress that hid some kind of pocket.

She looked at him again. "Let's go," she said.

They followed in the wake of the guards. The white dress could not be hidden, but with the red belt gone, she appeared normal enough and passed for an average citizen. He kept hold of the staff.

The guards were well out of sight. Behind, the other troop of guards must have stopped at the Haranast. There was no one near them now except the usual citizens of Esgallien. The people were less desperate than they were before, but not by much, and he knew the streets were no longer safe. Too many eyes were on them; too many that might have seen what Erlissa had done. And it only took one to report it to the first guard that they saw.

He took her hand once more. "Time to disappear," he said.

Without seeming to hasten, he led her off the Hainer Lon. Several people watched them go, but no one followed. He made sure of that.

When they were several streets away and the crowds were normal once more, he put his arms around her and picked her up, swinging her in a full circle. When he put her down, he kissed her hard on the lips.

She kissed him back. A few long moments it lasted, both oblivious to anything else, and then he let her go.

She looked at him. "So, you missed me, then?"

"You bet I did."

They moved on down the street, but now they walked arm in arm and she leaned against him as they went.

"Where to?" she asked.

"An alley," he said. "One that's dark and quiet."

She looked at him strangely, and he laughed.

"We need to hide," he said. "Although privacy wouldn't hurt either. I've discovered a good way to get off the streets, but we have to stay clear of windows."

She gave him another strange look, but he kept on walking. He did not want to tell her about what had happened to him this morning.

They wandered through the streets. As they headed away from the Hainer Lon it grew less crowded, but he would have to find a very quiet alley indeed for what he intended to do during daylight hours.

The roofs were a good place to hide. They offered views of the city streets, and no one would look for them there, but to get on top of one was the hard part. The climbing was difficult, and most of all to be seen trying to get there was to risk being taken as a thief and having the City Watch called. Yet, if he could find a place quiet enough, they could disappear that way. And disappear they must, for it was far too dangerous at the moment. Also, it would give them a chance to talk and to work out what they intended to do next.

The streets grew narrow and winding. They were passing into one of the poorer areas of the city. The buildings rose tall and gray about them, like cliff faces overlooking a dark river that ran between steep banks.

Rubbish, both old and recently discarded, lay everywhere, and they picked their path carefully. Lanrik loved the city, but some parts were an eyesore, and dangerous as well. He would not normally come to an area like this, especially with a girl, but it served a purpose now.

It was not only the buildings and streets that were different. The people had changed too. There were few markets, few friendly eyes, but many dirty children playing in the corners. And men and women who stared at them suspiciously.

Lanrik realized that he and Erlissa, for all their recent troubles, were well dressed. Far too well dressed for a poor neighborhood like this.

He had better find what he wanted quickly, or they were at just as much risk of being robbed as they were of discovery by Royal Guards.

He turned down each narrow street that he could find, and this seemed to bring him to the kind of place that he wanted. They were now come to a maze of winding lanes and very narrow alleys. He walked past a few, but kept on going as there were people in each one, though not many. After a while, he came to one that was empty. It was also dark, smelly, and filled with the rubbish of long years of neglect.

"Just what I'm looking for," he said.

Erlissa looked ahead with some distaste, but did not answer.

They walked into the alley, and he kept a close eye on things. No one followed them. No one was ahead of them at the far end, either. And as best as he could see, no one looked out of the few narrow windows that had a view of them.

149

"Here," he said.

It was another drainpipe, like the one that he had climbed last night. Only this time it would not be necessary to ascend very far. It led up only one story, and it came straight out of a windowless brick wall. However, there was a balcony next to it, and the pipe would give them access to its small roof. Above that again, the real roof of the building was within reach.

"You want me to climb that?" Erlissa did not look happy about the situation.

"I'll push you up from behind," he said. "It won't take long. Just be careful not to make too much noise when you step on the balcony's roof."

She frowned, but reached up to take hold of the drainpipe. It did not take long for her to climb, and he did not have to offer much help. When she was on the roof, he handed her the staff and made the climb himself.

There was noise now; the sound of scuffing boots and muffled talk, and they both hunkered down low and went still. Someone was close by, but it appeared to be a group of people in the nearby street, rather than the alley. The sounds soon drifted away.

"Quickly," he said. "We're too easily seen here."

They stood up on the balcony and Erlissa reached for the real roof above it. She deftly pulled herself up so that her head was above it, and then with a final heave she slithered her whole body over the rim and disappeared from sight.

A moment later he followed. He looked around and was satisfied that he had chosen well. There were no windows in the other buildings high enough to look out onto this roof. They should be safe here, at least for a while, until they could figure out what to do next.

Unexpectedly, she put her arms around him and gave him a kiss.

"I thought I'd lost you," she whispered.

Lanrik looked her straight in the eye. "I'm hard to kill. Especially when I have so much to live for."

"So I've noticed." She rested her head on his shoulder. "Now, tell me what happened."

He explained to her how the charred-man had pursued him, leaving out that he had ensured that it did so, and of his final ploy in the city aqueduct.

She asked him several questions about the specifics of its reaction to water. Neither of them could be certain if that was a weakness in Ebona's witchery, or if the creature's ungainliness simply meant that it could not swim.

"It won't give up the hunt," Lanrik said.

"No. Ebona has done something to it. I mean, apart from the obvious. It's driven to find us. Tormented every moment that it doesn't. But at least now I'm prepared if it finds us again."

Lanrik was not so confident. He had seen it struck by lòhren-fire, and even that most deadly form of lòhrengai had proved ineffective. Erlissa would need to think of something else.

"So," she said after a pause. "The creature just chased you? I don't believe it. *You* did something to make that happen, didn't you?"

Lanrik looked away. He did not want to answer, but he did not want to lie to her, either.

She put a hand over his. "We're in this together. No more splitting up. No more *anything* by ourselves. Well do what we have to do in Esgallien, and we'll do it together. Even if it means fighting the charred-man, or anyone else that we must. And when we're done, we'll get out of here and meet Aranloth."

151

He was not surprised that she had worked out that the creature had followed him at his own instigation. What surprised him, even impressed him, was that although she was upset that he had taken that risk for her, she did not make a point of saying so. Instead, she just made sure that he understood that there was only one way forward for them now, whatever happened.

"All right. We're in this together. No matter what."

She patted his hand. "Now, what do we do next?"

It was a good question, and Lanrik had no easy answer. They discussed a few more details, such as how she had evaded capture during the night and where she had gotten her disguise. And then he mentioned the park and the guards surrounding it.

"Conhain's Rest," she said. "Now, that really *is* strange."

"There was just no reason for them to be there," he added.

"And yet, there must be."

He raised his palms. "I can't figure it out."

She tapped her fingers against the staff. "I think it's just too much of a coincidence."

"What do you mean?"

"Conhain was Ebona's worst enemy. It was by Aranloth that her power was broken when Esgallien was founded, and yet without Conhain, the people would have fallen under her sway. It was their love for him that won out – a feeling that she could never inspire."

"But that was nearly a thousand years ago. What could Conhain have to do with things now? She killed him, or her dogs did, anyway."

"Yes. She killed him, but her hatred did not die with the deed."

"I don't understand."

152

She looked at him. "There's a reason that no one knows where Conhain is buried. There's a reason there are so many rumors, but so little truth on the subject."

"I've heard it said," replied Lanrik, "that he might be buried in the park. I've heard lots of things said, but I still don't understand what any of it has to do with Ebona. Or the guards who surround the park."

"Everything, or nothing. I'm not sure, but I know this, for Aranloth told me himself. When our ancestors founded the city, there was an ever-present risk of treason and corruption. Some remained who would conspire with our enemies, especially those who once had served Ebona. Her influence was broken, and theirs along with it, yet it was feared that out of spite they might desecrate Conhain's grave. They had sworn to do so." She paused, taking her time to consider what she would say next.

"And of course," she continued, "there was also a chance that others, less hateful, but more greedy, would plunder the tomb. Much that Conhain owned was interred with him, and most of his possessions were gifted to him by the Halathrin. There are treasures inside his tomb beyond the wealth or craft of humanity."

Lanrik had thought he knew the history of the city, but it was clear that even the Raithlin had gaps in their lore.

"So *that's* why no one knows where he was buried. It makes sense," he said.

"It was Aranloth's plan. But a few do know, have always known, where he was buried. A few who guard the tomb, who keep watch on things, and make sure his sleep is not disturbed."

"So Conhain really *does* rest in the park?"

She nodded. "Yes. But think, Lanrik, there's more."

He closed his eyes and considered all that she had said. That someone, or some group, guarded it through the years was key. Whoever they were, they would be trusted.

He opened his eyes. "The Lindrath," he said. "Not just the present one, but all the Raithlindrath's from the founding. Who would be better trusted to keep the secret and watch over things?"

She nodded. "Yes. And your Lindrath was the last to hold that secret. He learned it from his predecessor, and he knows also that the tomb is shielded. Not just watched by himself, but protected. For Aranloth himself built the tomb, and he set forces to work there to guard against Ebona and her allies, knowing that although her power was broken, she would one day return. Conhain's tomb is the one place in Esgallien that she cannot go, that she cannot destroy, nor have men destroy for her. For ùhrengai, the same sort of force that protects Lòrenta, infuses it."

Lanrik ran a hand through his hair. "So you think that when the Lindrath escaped, he went there for protection?"

"Yes. It makes sense. He's in the tomb, and the guards are there to ensure he doesn't escape. For while they cannot get in, likewise, he cannot get out, and must die of thirst or hunger, eventually."

Lanrik shrugged. "If I know the Lindrath, and if what you think is really true, they'll be waiting a long time, for he'll have stockpiled supplies there. If not before, then certainly after Ebona came to the city."

She raised her eyebrows. "I didn't think of that. I hope you're right."

Lanrik let out a sigh. "None of this really makes sense, though. If the tomb is protected, how could he get inside it? And if he did, why are they guarding the whole park? They could save enormous expense and manpower by just surrounding the tomb."

"The tomb is protected. But there *is* a way in, for those who know. Just as there's a way into Lòrenta. And you're assuming that he's trapped in there. What if there were tunnels, leading out in any direction, finding their exit in any part of the park? Ebona could not know where. They would have to guard everywhere."

"*Are* there tunnels?"

Erlissa shrugged. "I don't know. And neither could Ebona. Aranloth only mentioned these things to me in passing. It was just something that lòhrens should know, he never went into detail."

Lanrik thought about it all. No matter which way he looked at it, it was plausible. The thing that confirmed it to him was the number of guards. So many of them. So much expense. Nothing could justify that except the prospect of capturing the Lindrath, or ensuring his death.

"I think you're right," he said at last.

"I do, too. But what are we going to do about it?"

"The only thing we can. The one thing that the Lindrath needs most. The one thing that Ebona wants the least. We have to rescue him."

Erlissa looked at him. Her eyes had widened, and he saw many things there, including outright fear. But he did not see unwillingness.

"You always come up with the boldest of ideas," she said. "But tell me, how can we do it? He's guarded by what must amount to most of Esgallien's army. How can we possibly get in there, let alone get out again?"

Lanrik rubbed his chin. "There'll be a way. Let me think on it."

"Oh, I don't doubt there's a way. And I don't doubt you'll discover it. And it'll be sure to be something so breathtaking in its audacity, so outright crazy, that it just might work."

He winked at her. "Well, you know all about that sort of thing. You pulled off something like that yourself just earlier. Who else but you would, or even could, impersonate the Witch-queen?"

Erlissa grinned. "She'll be annoyed when she learns of that …"

"*Very* annoyed. And yet, I can live quite easily with her discomfit."

He sat back, more serious now. "All right, I have an idea. But if we try it, we'll pass far beyond our arrangement with Aranloth. We'll not just be learning of all that's going on in the city – we'll be actively defying Ebona, and there may be consequences to that."

"Yes, but we've already gone beyond our original mission. Circumstances made us. Aranloth won't like it, but he'll understand."

Erlissa tilted her head after she spoke the lòhren's name, and Lanrik saw a look of concern cross her face. It passed after a moment, and she looked back at him.

"So, tell me. What's this idea of yours?"

15. The Boldest of the Bold

It was a long afternoon. The sun beat down upon the roof, and there was no shade. They dozed fitfully, coming alert at the slightest sound, but few people entered the alley, and those who did were oblivious to the fugitives hiding above them.

At length, dusk came to the city. Dark shadows crept into the alleys and lanes, and the air cooled. But the tiles did not. They remained hot and uncomfortable.

Of one thing, Lanrik was grateful. He had not seen any soldiers or guards. Had the search for them moved to another part of the city? There was no way to know. But he was sick and tired of hiding.

When the sun had set, and even the glow of it had disappeared from the horizon, he woke Erlissa. It was time to dare the streets once more.

The plan that he had conceived would work equally well during the day or night, but having come to the conclusion that the Lindrath was in the park, he wanted to reach him as quickly as possible. He needed help, and they would bring it to him without delay. At least, they would try.

But Lanrik had no illusions that his plan was not risky. More risky even than infiltrating an enemy army. For this time, his skills as a Raithlin would be near useless.

They slipped down from their hiding place without noise or problem. Nevertheless, when they reached the alley, Lanrik gave Erlissa her staff and drew his sword.

Royal Guards were not the only thing to fear, and they were in just as much danger from thieves and ruffians.

They began to move through the lanes and alleys, heading back toward the inner city and the Hainer Lon. It was quiet all about them. There were no nighttime revelers. The streets seemed hushed, even brooding.

Esgallien was effectively a conquered nation, and yet he had seen signs that its people were ready to reclaim their freedom. He felt it now as he walked through the empty streets. It was *too* quiet. And not the quiet of fear. Anger and resentment festered. Like a living thing, it wandered the streets with them. It occupied every house and every tenement building that they passed. It was the heartbeat of Esgallien.

Things must have been subdued after the Raithlin had left. But now word was spreading of a new Raithlin in the city, and the Witch-queen's efforts to find him. That had reawakened their spirit. He just hoped that it did not get them killed.

Something made him suddenly wary, and he slowed and placed himself in front of Erlissa. For a few moments, he stood still and silent. Nothing happened. And then he caught the glint of naked steel.

A group of three men emerged from the shadows. They had heard him and Erlissa coming, perhaps were even waiting here for victims. There was no doubt that they were thieves. And yet they were not prepared for a man with his sword already drawn. A man who stood his ground, without sign of fear, and that was ready for them.

They exchanged glances among themselves. Dim figures in the shadows though they were, he read the will to attack in them. But doubt vied with it.

He continued to gaze at them coolly, saying nothing, but regarding them with indifference. That made a greater statement than any words he could say.

The long moments passed, and then the group lost their nerve. This was too risky for them. It was something beyond the usual, and their knives were no match for a sword, though they held three blades to his one.

The men backed away, and then hastened down the street. Lanrik watched them until they were out of sight. And then he listened carefully. He heard their steps break into a full run.

Erlissa chuckled. "I'd have run too, had the look on your face been directed at me."

"What look?"

"The one that said, *I don't care if you live or die. I just don't want to nick my sword on your bones.*"

Lanrik grinned in the dark. "That's a useful look to have. Sometimes it saves a lot of problems."

They moved ahead. The streets grew wider once more, and people were more frequent. But it was an eerie night, as though the city was waiting for something. Lanrik did not like it. It only added to the pressure, for what they must soon attempt was so dangerous, so filled with risk and the potential for disaster, that his nerves were already on edge.

He concentrated instead on the intended result. If they were successful, they would have the one thing that even Aranloth dared not hope for. The Lindrath. His information about the city and the Witch-queen would be priceless. And that did not even take into account the personal side of things. The Lindrath was good man, a man who had tutored him, taught him, guided him like a father, and been there for him through many troubles. He was the closest thing that Lanrik had to family, saving his uncle. And during much of the time that he had known the Lindrath, he had thought his uncle was dead.

Lanrik put these thoughts from his mind as well. He must think only of the task ahead, and how best to perform it, rather than the possible consequences.

They went as close as they could to the park before they stepped out onto the Hainer Lon. Just before they did, he paused for a moment.

"Are you sure you want to do this? There's no backing out once we start."

"I'm sure. If things go wrong – they go wrong."

He looked at her a while, and she returned his gaze. There was no other like her in all Esgallien. Perhaps all Alithoras. She had courage, intelligence, determination. She wielded power that he could not quite comprehend, and her strength was increasing month by month. She was little more than a lòhren in training, and yet she already had her staff, and the land had called upon her, put her through enormous trials, and she had come out the other end. Truly, she was one of a kind, and he would rather face trouble with her than anyone else that he knew.

He winked at her. "To luck," he said.

She winked back. "To luck."

They moved along the Hainer Lon. The park was on their right now, the ring of soldiers still there, lining the way and continuing into the darkness.

Lanrik stayed in the shadows as long as he could, but when he saw what he wanted, a captain of the Royal Guard inspecting the line, the time had come.

He stepped out into the light, Erlissa by his side, and walked straight toward the man. He made no effort to conceal himself, or to draw a weapon. His mission tonight was one of words. They were his weapon. They would see him win or lose the quest.

Surprisingly, they reached the captain without being challenged. Neither he nor the soldiers paid them any attention.

Lanrik came to a standstill, only a few paces away. Finally, the captain looked at him.

"It's your lucky night," Lanrik said.

The captain stared at him blankly at first, and then irritation crossed his face. His gaze shifted to Erlissa, and then back to him. And then the look of irritation swiftly turned to one of wide-eyed fear and excitement.

The man drew his sword. Lanrik stood motionless.

"Good. You know who we are. But you won't need that. Not if you truly serve Ebona."

The captain screamed out. "To me! To me!"

The soldiers up and down the line seemed surprised, and he kept on screaming until about thirty of them broke away from their watch and came over.

"It's them!" the captain yelled.

"Of course it's us," Lanrik said. "Who else?"

"Take them!" the captain ordered.

The soldiers hesitated. Some of them had realized who they were, but their heart was not in the pursuit as much as those of the Royal Guard's. They moved in slowly.

Lanrik drew his sword. The soldiers stilled. Even the captain stopped shouting. A moment Lanrik held it in his hand, and then he casually tossed it to the ground at the man's feet.

"A sign of goodwill," he said. "You need no soldiers now. We're on the same side again."

"Which side is that?" asked the captain.

"Ebona's, naturally. We've agreed to serve her, and just in time, it appears."

The soldiers remained still. Lanrik thought that many of them looked at him in disappointment, at least those out of view of the captain.

"Do you expect me to believe that?"

"Of course. Why else would we come to you? Why else would I disarm myself? Only idiots would do that, unless we were on a mission – one given to us by Ebona herself. One that she is most interested in seeing succeed."

The captain was not convinced. "Then why isn't she with you?"

"A good question. You can ask her yourself, if you care to, when she arrives shortly."

"Where is she?"

"She's dealing with a little problem at the moment. It seems the lòhren Aranloth is in the city as well. She'll be along soon to sort all this out."

"Then we'll just wait here, all together and nice and cozy, until she does."

Lanrik raised an eyebrow. "Really? Well, that's fine by me. Although I rather think she might hope to see more progress when she arrives."

"Progress at what?"

"In capturing the Lindrath, of course. What else did you think this was about?"

"And what can you possibly do that thousands of soldiers couldn't?"

Lanrik maintained his nonchalant attitude, but his heart raced at the confirmation that the captain had just provided. The Lindrath really *was* here.

"Tsk, tsk. You really have to ask? I'm not sure Ebona is going to be happy with you."

"Stop calling her Ebona. She's the *queen*."

"You can call her queen if you like. She's Ebona to me. I knew her long before she came to the city, you know."

"Well, you still haven't answered me. What can you do that an army cannot?"

Lanrik sighed. "For starters, I can get into Conhain's tomb, the place where he's hiding. I'm a Raithlin, after all. And I'm his friend besides. I can convince him to come out with me; a thing that you cannot. And I rather think that Ebona would like to see that. She has questions for him."

"I'm sure she does. So what am I supposed to do? Just let you walk in there and come back with a prisoner in your own good time?"

Lanrik shook his head. "Of course not. I didn't really expect you to trust me. But you have my sword. You have us surrounded. Bring as many men as you think you need to ensure your safety, and come along with us. It shouldn't take too long."

The captain stared at him. Lanrik read doubt on the man's face, but he read fear there as well. Fear of Ebona, and having to answer to her if his choices were not in line with her expectations. If he delayed things, it might cost him his life. If he went ahead as suggested, well, what could really go wrong?

The captain came to his decision. He gave orders, and twenty soldiers formed a circle around them.

"Really? Twenty men? Should I be flattered, or insulted?"

"Let's just get this over with."

"As you wish."

Lanrik did not hesitate. He walked into the park, Erlissa by his side, and the twenty-man guard. He felt a pang as he left the sword behind on the grass, but there was no way to take it back. They would not let him, and if he tried, it would make them suspicious. At least this way, unarmed and at their mercy, he had control of the situation. The irony of that thought made him laugh out loud.

"Something amusing?" asked the captain.

"Many things," replied Lanrik. "Many things. But mostly this: isn't life strange? Yesterday and today, you were chasing me. But now you give me an honor guard so that I can fulfill Ebona's greatest desire."

"It's not an honor guard!"

"It's not? Well, if it isn't now, it will be when she arrives. You won't want to miss out on being the captain that helped me get her the Lindrath. Not if you ever wish to be more than captain."

The man did not answer, and Lanrik knew he had him just where he wanted him. He was still suspicious, as any man must be, and yet he now mostly believed the story.

They walked through the park, crossing near the grove of trees where he had seen the fox last night. He wondered where it was. Probably safe and secure somewhere, if he knew foxes.

It was different in the park than in the city. He felt more at home here. It was as though he was in the wilderness, and the park, especially at night, were assets to him. Not so much the soldiers, should it come to a confrontation. His plan hinged on avoiding that, though.

Away in the city he heard a dog bark, and then another. It was not a sound of the wilderness, for where there were no men, there were no dogs. He was more used to the howling of wolves, the yelping of foxes, and the harsh and drawn out hawing of aurochs in the swamps.

Dew wetted the grass, and they left a trail on the lawn that a drunk tracker, wearing a blindfold, could follow.

He did not mind. Tonight was not a night for hiding. That was no more his plan than fighting.

They moved toward the center of the park without speaking. Conhain's tomb was in the monument constructed there. It did not look like a tomb. Nor did it even look like there was any sort of entry to the inside of it. Rather, it looked to be just what everybody thought it was: a monument to the founding of Esgallien. Yet, evidently, it was more than it seemed.

The stars shone palely from above, their brightness diffused by the lights of the city. All was quiet. Nothing stirred. Even here, there was a sense of brooding. He felt prickles on the back of his neck as he sometimes did in the wilderness when there was no one else for hundreds of miles, and yet he had the sense of being watched. He dismissed it. Now was not a time for nerves.

They did not go near the wells that he had used to escape the charred-man, but they passed by the area. They went deeper into the park, where there were several patches of forest, though they did not enter them. Moving between different groves, they came to a gentle slope. They could not see their destination yet, the dark was too deep and the starlight too pale, but at the slope's crest was the monument.

They were now far enough away from the rest of the city that there barely seemed any noise. They were alone here – he and Erlissa, the one Royal Guard and the twenty soldiers. He looked back at the captain, and saw his unease. And uneasy he should be. He had not quite counted on this. Twenty men had seemed excessive at the Hainer Lon. Not so much now. If it had been possible, he would have brought his own kind, twenty Royal Guards. That made Lanrik grin. The Royal Guards were busy searching the city for *him*, and consequently spread very thinly through the lines around the park. It was upon that fact that his plan hinged.

The captain stared back hard at him, and he looked away. He was not ready to set things in motion yet. Let the captain grow more nervous, and let the soldiers see what lay ahead.

"There it is," Erlissa said.

She was right. The monument had come into view. He had seen it many times, but it looked different now. He realized what else it looked like, and it was another confirmation of the information that Erlissa had given him. It was a structure dominated by triangles, that strange architecture favored by the Letharn. He had seen it in their tombs and the building that gave entry to them. Only Aranloth would know, or favor, that style; so it *was* constructed under his direction. That was the final proof, and he had no doubt that inside the first and greatest king of Esgallien lay buried.

They approached the monument. Just before it was a stone-lined pond, filled with water. A man-high statue rose from its center. It was Conhain, though it was a younger version than what was often seen. Here, he wore no sword and rode no warhorse, but he looked about him, a long-dead sense of wonder on his boyish face. Something about it reminded Lanrik of Aranloth's statue in Lòrenta.

Unlike the building that the lòhren had used to enter the tombs of the Letharn, this one was not enclosed by walls. Instead, tall pillars held up the massive roof, and the stone floor beneath was open to wind and light, but not rain.

They were close enough now to see the carvings, for the triangular gables and the tall pillars were decorated with images of the great battle that marked the founding of the city. Conhain was there, and his warhorse. And

166

the Red Cloth of Victory. So too Ebona, and her dogs, and the elug army that the first Esgalliens had fought. And there were Raithlin too.

Lanrik's steps echoed hollowly on the stone floor when he crossed it. The soldiers seemed curious, looking about them at the carved pillars and colored mosaics beneath their feet. Their wide eyes took in a scene that they must have observed many times before, but they viewed things now in the new light that the king, the great king at the heart of everything Esgallien stood for, was buried here.

The captain appeared less impressed. "Are you sure this is the place?"

"Yes, Captain."

"I see no tomb here. I see no doors or entryways to anything."

Erlissa answered him. "It wouldn't have stayed undiscovered if it showed those things openly. But there *is* a door."

She walked to the very center of the floor. Here was a monument within a monument. A square structure stood there, built of stone and intricately carved. It rose ten feet high, and was ten feet wide and long. Yet its top was angled to a point on each side, a top that formed four triangles.

Lanrik smiled. Once again, this was confirmation that they were in the right place. It would have looked right at home anywhere among the old constructions of the Letharn.

Erlissa examined the square structure. The captain, in turn, studied Erlissa. Lanrik knew the time had come to distract him.

"So," he said. "Has Ebona been good to you?"

"What do you mean?"

"Have you been promoted under her?"

"What business is that of yours?"

"Well, I suppose that's a yes. You don't really seem old enough for your rank, though. Or experienced enough, for that matter. But you do seem – how shall I put it, *vile* enough."

Some of the soldiers sniggered, and the captain was about to reply, but at just that moment light flashed behind them and a deep tremor thrummed in the stone beneath them.

They all turned to look at Erlissa. She had opened a door into the square block, and inside, a stairwell led down into the dark.

"Hold on!" the captain said to Lanrik. "What's she doing? I thought *you* were the one who knew how to open it?"

Lanrik smiled. "Things are sometimes not as they seem, Captain. For instance, I'm unarmed and at your mercy. But I can still—"

Without warning Lanrik struck. It was a blow so unexpected, so swift and forceful, that his fist against the man's skull sounded like a whip crack in the park.

The captain, taken by surprise, toppled to the ground. Lanrik had thought it would have taken several punches, but he had the feeling that the captain had never been struck before. He lay on the floor, still and unconscious. When he woke, he would have a headache and a throbbing chin.

Lanrik stepped back a few paces to where Erlissa stood at the entrance of the tomb. The soldiers seemed in shock, not having ever expected this. Some, however, had drawn their swords.

Now was the great gamble, and the crux of Lanrik's plan. He looked at them.

"Well, men. I'm a Raithlin. Did you really think that I would serve the Witch-queen?"

The soldiers did not answer, but he saw on some faces signs of relief, and that encouraged him. The Raithlin were held in high honor, and he had not disappointed them.

"The Witch-queen rules for now," he said. "But other forces are at work. The lòhrens have not abandoned Esgallien to her. Nor the Raithlin. In time, she will be overthrown."

"It doesn't seem likely," said one of the men.

"Doesn't it? Then why is she scared?" Lanrik asked. "Why else would she have so many guard against the escape of the Lindrath?"

He paused. He did not wish to start a debate with them. Instead, he must speak from the heart, and tell them truths.

"The moment of choice for all Esgallien is soon to come," he continued. "The moment where we must take sides. We must fight for our home. Or we must fight for the Witch-queen. For you, that moment of choice is now."

He looked around at them. Doubt and confusion filled their faces. And the fear that Ebona had instilled in them.

"Now, you can walk away from here, disappear into the city and wait and prepare for the help that is coming. Or stand against me, the last Raithlin, about to rescue the last Lindrath, at the tomb of Conhain. For truthfully, he *does* lie here. Will you give your alliance to the Witch-queen, or to Conhain's memory?"

The stars twinkled above. A cold breeze blew. The captain stirred and groaned on the stone floor. The soldiers looked at each other, and then turned to Lanrik.

16. Not Death, or the Oblivion of the Ages...

Lanrik waited. Erlissa stood next to him. At their back was the entrance to a tomb. Before them were the men who would decide what happened next.

And those men looked uneasy. He was asking much of them, for their lives were at risk. Then again, they were a randomly chosen group of soldiers. The captain would not even know their names.

"I choose Conhain," said one of the men.

There were murmurs of agreement. Another man spoke loudly.

"A pox on the Witch-queen's face!"

A ripple of laughter flowed through the group. Lanrik let out a long breath. He knew these type of men. He knew *soldiers*. They might be rough at times, but their hearts were in the right place. And every child growing up in Esgallien played at being Conhain. He was revered. Still, it was a gamble such as he had never taken before.

"The Lindrath needs me," Lanrik said. "And Esgallien needs you. We must part here, but I won't forget what you've done. Not ever."

"And we won't forget the Raithlin," said one of the men. "They helped many in the city, and the Witch-queen made them suffer for it." He paused. "I have a feeling you're going to make her pay for that."

"Her time is coming," Lanrik answered.

He bent down to the captain and took his sword. For a moment he looked at the men, and they looked at him.

There was a strange feeling between them. A sense of camaraderie among strangers.

He removed his empty sheath, buckled on the new blade and then took Erlissa's hand. They turned to the opening of the tomb.

A set of stairs ran down at a steep angle into darkness. They followed them, taking each step carefully, and a sense of awe thickened the air. Conhain was near, and though even his bones might now be dust, he was still *Conhain*: the man who had given his life for his people; the king who forged victory from despair.

Erlissa slowed. A faint light sprang from the end of her staff.

"You judged the soldiers well," she said. "In truth, I thought they would be too scared to let us go."

"They *were* scared," Lanrik answered. "But you and I have both been there before. It doesn't mean not doing the right thing."

"But if they didn't?"

He shrugged. "Then like we discussed earlier, we would have been forced into hiding with the Lindrath, or into fighting our way free."

"But you never thought, not for a second, that we would actually have to do that?"

"I know these kind of men. I'm one of them. They have no will to serve the Witch-queen, and perhaps even less to answer to some captain, promoted above his ability because he *will* serve her. That would not go down well with them. And to see him humbled, a man of arrogance and borrowed power, and to be reminded of Conhain at the same time, the pinnacle of humility and sacrifice – well, I don't think I left them much choice."

Erlissa raised her eyebrows, but did not answer.

"So you *didn't* believe the plan would work?"

She grinned at him. "No, I didn't."

"Then why did you go along with it?"

"Because *you* believed in it. That was enough for me."

She took the lead and walked ahead, the faint light of her staff wavering in the darkness.

Lanrik followed her, amazed at what she had just said.

The stairs ceased. They had reached a near-bare chamber. The walls bore carvings, strange shapes that moved and writhed in the wavering light. Lanrik felt a sense of dread. This was altogether too much like the tombs of the Letharn. But there were no harakgar here to guard it. And yet, Erlissa had said that *something* guarded it. He felt it, too. A force that probed his mind, tested his innermost thoughts. It reminded him of the ùhrengai at the fountain in Lòrenta.

She paused, and the light of her staff stilled, glowing faint but steady.

"I can sense Aranloth's touch all around us. His power is so refined, so skilled, that even after all these years it sings his name." She hesitated. "But there are other forces too. Some that I don't understand."

She moved to the nearest wall and studied a carving. It was Conhain again, but this time not as a youth. He held high the Red Cloth of Victory. Erlissa peered at the writing above him. It was in a strange and archaic script, but they both knew what it said. She whispered the words.

Nothing lasts forever. Not men, nor chiefs … nor even cities.

"Fitting words for a tomb," he said. "But why is the room empty?"

Erlissa frowned. "I think this is a decoy. Great forces protect the tomb, and yet Aranloth seldom takes chances. An intruder, reaching this far, might conclude that someone had already looted the place. They might not look for a second chamber, but there is one."

They searched around, studying the carvings and floor for any hint of a hidden door. Erlissa stopped for a long time in one place, and Lanrik went over to join her.

"More script," she said. "This time in Halathrin."

He peered at it, but his understanding of the immortal's tongue was not as good as hers, and she read it out.

Eleth nar duril.

She did not translate it. She did not need to. They both remembered the phrase from when Aranloth last spoke it near Lake Alithorin, when they found the ancient Halathrin slain by Shurilgar's sorcery. It was a phrase from their funerary rites.

"Lie in peace," he murmured.

"Fitting once again, for a tomb," Erlissa said. "But why is it written in Halathrin and not our own speech?"

"I suppose," Lanrik answered, "that it makes sense. Conhain was a great friend of the Halathrin."

He thought about it further. "The image below the writing fits in as well, almost as though it's emphasizing the point."

Erlissa traced the carving, an image of Conhain reclining as though asleep, with her fingertips.

"Yes, it fits in *too* well, but you wouldn't see the connection unless you could read Halathrin script."

She traced the outline again, but this time faint blue light flickered beneath her fingertips. When she finished, a sudden white light sprang from the carving in response, and a silvery image of Conhain hung in the very air.

Erlissa spoke again, her voice clear and loud.

Eleth nar duril.

The stone of the chamber about them thrummed. A great slab shuddered to their right. It pulsed with light, and then by some force of lòhrengai it twisted at an angle and slid back, leaving an opening.

"A tomb within a tomb," Erlissa said.

She moved to go forward, but Lanrik rested a hand on her shoulder.

"The Lindrath should be somewhere in there. I'll go first."

He moved ahead, standing for a while near the opening until his eyes adjusted. It was deep and dark inside the next room. Erlissa's light did not go far inside.

Lanrik drew the sword that he had taken from the captain. He did not like it. The balance was wrong, and the hilt felt awkward in his hand.

"Lindrath!" he called. "It's Lanrik. I'm coming in."

A voice answered from the dark. "Come slowly. And if you're pretending to be Lanrik, don't come at all – not unless you want a sword buried in your belly."

Lanrik laughed. He knew the Lindrath's voice, even if it sounded hollow and weary. Hope surged in him. But now was not a time for unnecessary risk. He stepped ahead slowly, the sword blade lowered, but not sheathed.

He moved cautiously, being sure that each pace made a noise so that the Lindrath would know that he was not trying to sneak in.

When he stepped through the doorway the light from Erlissa's staff flared brighter, and the whole room came into view. It was smaller than the previous one, but it was not empty.

All manner of things lay heaped on the floor or stood against the walls. He cast his gaze around in wonder. Coins and jewels glittered in the light. The dulled and dust-covered blades of swords and spear-points still showed keen edges. Some were no doubt precious heirlooms, things of ceremony and pomp. But others, broken, shattered or bloody, had once been held by hands in battle. There also he saw carnyx horns, the man-high instruments of bronze that winded an

174

unearthly moan. They had lain silent through the long centuries.

He knew that he looked upon the remnants of that *first* of battles. It was as though time had taken him back to the founding of Esgallien. He knew Conhain's name, but what heroes had held these things, fought and died alongside their king, that the memory of a nation had forgotten?

These swords, these shields, these spears – rusted, pitted things of tarnished steel and worm-eaten wood, were in their own way a memorial. His heart raced, and he gave thanks to the unknown warriors. Conhain had not saved his people single-handedly.

He looked to the walls. Carvings decorated them. He saw scenes of battle. He saw Ebona. He saw too, in a far corner, many Raithlin. Their cloaks and hoods were unmistakable. So also their short swords, the trotting fox emblem etched into the blades. But something below them drew his eye. There lay the long decayed skeletons of four massive dogs.

Lanrik shuddered. These were the very hounds that had killed Conhain. He looked upon matters of legend, things of a past so ancient that it would be old even to Aranloth. And it was fitting that the bones lay beneath the Raithlin. For it was the Raithlin who had hunted the dogs and killed them after Conhain's death.

He gazed around, trying to ignore the wonder of it all. Two things he did not see, and that worried him. One was the Lindrath. The second was Conhain, or at least his sarcophagus.

He stopped and raised his sword. At that moment he heard a noise, and a figure sprang from the floor near his feet. Where before he had seen only dust and rags, now the Lindrath rose, his Raithlin cloak swirling, his Raithlin sword weaving in the air.

175

The two men looked at each other. A moment they stood frozen in place, a moment they appeared ready to strike, neither trusting in the possibility of the other. And then slowly, the Lindrath lowered the point of his blade.

"Is it really you?"

Lanrik sheathed his sword.

"It's good to see you."

The Lindrath dropped his weapon. It clattered loudly on the stone. He stepped forward and hugged Lanrik, and Lanrik hugged him back.

For a while they did not move, but eventually the Lindrath stood away.

"I didn't think to ever see a living soul again. It's been too long."

Lanrik looked at him. "Why didn't you try to escape? You might have done it, at night."

"Oh, don't worry. I thought about it. I even scouted the park a few times in the beginning. I could've slipped through, all right. But why should I? I was safe here. I had food. And when I saw the effort they were making to ensure that I didn't, I thought that I had no better way of vexing Ebona. There must be thousands of soldiers out there. But I suppose, when I ran out of food, I would've tried it."

"Do you know that the city thinks you're dead? Ebona had a body hung from the palace gate and claimed it was you."

The Lindrath looked subdued. "Another murder at the Witch-queen's hands. I tell you, hundreds, maybe even thousands, have died. And her power grows with each death. It's as it was in the old stories. She must be stopped."

Erlissa stepped forward. "We *will* stop her."

The Lindrath eyed her. "You've come a long way since last we met," he said. "A very long way indeed."

He turned back to Lanrik. "And so have you. I hear tell of a new order of Raithlin. I'm glad to see the old skills being taught. There are few left now who know them. Only me in Esgallien, and a few survivors fled to Galenthern."

"Help is at hand," Lanrik said. "Aranloth is on the move, and the lòhrens with him. He won't allow Ebona to hold sway for long, and nether will we."

They would have said more, but at that moment a deep noise boomed. It sounded like an iron-shod staff striking the stone floor of the tomb. Thrice it echoed all about them, and they looked around confused.

"Where did *that* come from?" Lanrik asked.

"I don't know," the Lindrath answered.

Erlissa straightened. Her face was pale, and she gripped her staff tightly.

"I do." There was a strange light in her eyes, part amazement, part fear. She raised the staff and pointed with it to the wall opposite the entrance.

"It came from in there."

The Lindrath went white. "It cannot be."

"It was," she said. "I heard it. And we both know there is yet a third room."

Lanrik glanced from one to the other. "What third room?"

The Lindrath, his face drawn and haggard from his ordeal, spoke in a low voice.

"This is a tomb, Lanrik. But no body rests here." He waved an arm around. "These were some of Conhain's possessions, and those of his friends. But there is, as Erlissa says, a third room. Each Raithlindrath learns that from their predecessor. Each time the leadership changes, there's a secret ceremony here, in this very place, in front of the door to that other room. But none has ever opened it." He looked at Erlissa. "That's a secret kept among the Lindraths for a thousand years. No one else knew it."

Erlissa returned his gaze. "No one else knew it, save the lòhrens. For it was Aranloth who gave the first Lindrath the permission and knowledge to enter here."

Thrice more the boom sounded. A hollow noise from the tomb of the dead. When it stilled, the quiet was so deep that it felt like a weight upon them.

"Whatever causes it, we must discover," Erlissa said. She walked over to the far wall.

The others followed her. "You would dare to open it?" the Lindrath asked.

"Yes. For the noise means *something*. We must find out what."

"I don't like it," Lanrik said. "It's not our place to go in there."

"And yet we must," Erlissa said. "I feel it in my bones."

Lanrik did not argue with her. She sounded more like Aranloth every day, but he trusted her instincts.

"Then we have to hurry," he said. "We don't know what's happening outside, and we still have to escape. If the captain has woken, he might already be on his way to summon help."

"Or not," Erlissa said. "For to admit that we deceived him is likely to assure his death. And he knows it. But it will not take long to open the door. Though what will happen after that … I cannot say."

After a moment, she raised her staff and struck the wall with its tip. The sound echoed dully through the chamber. Thrice she struck, copying the noise that had drawn their attention. At the third stroke, a tongue of blue lòhrengai flickered from the walnut staff.

The lòhren-fire flared to life, and whatever enchantment hid the entry was revealed by its light, for now a blue flame, entwined with white, showed the edges of a door. A moment the lights flared, hurting their eyes in the dark, and then they sputtered out.

A door stood there, but not of stone. It was of ancient oak. On its other side rested the king, and whatever made the noise.

Erlissa hesitated only a moment, and then she opened it.

They looked into the third room: the tomb of Conhain that no man had seen in a thousand years. Lanrik's hair prickled.

There was no one there. No trapped Raithlin in hiding. No one off the street seeking refuge. No wild animal that had found a way in. No possible cause for the noise that they had heard.

But there were other things.

His gaze swept the room. There was little dust, merely a fine layer that filmed the surface of everything equally. The room was small. The skeleton of a massive horse lay on one side. On the other were books. Their pages seemed intact, and no doubt they were written in the Halathrin tongue, for Conhain was a scholar of that people.

On the back wall, fixed into the stone, protruded a spear. It was long. Its ash-wood shaft was polished by hands that had not held it, that had not lived, since Esgallien was a camp of vagabond wanderers. A shiver ran up his spine. Attached to the spear, hanging down in the still air, was the one symbol that every single person in Esgallien would recognize: the Red Cloth of Victory. Only this was not a symbol. It was the thing itself.

The cloth, once white, was steeped in the life-blood of Conhain. The stained and ragged material, somehow preserved in the dry air of the tomb, had been used to staunch the king's wounds and keep him alive a little longer. That same cloth, he later removed and swung down to signal the charge that defeated Esgallien's enemies. Lanrik felt tears blur his sight. Conhain had given so much for his people, sacrificed his happiness, even his life, for their benefit.

But even the cloth was insignificant compared to the one other thing in the room. A stone bier, four feet high and of polished marble, dominated its center. And there, laid out like the king he was, rested Conhain. He was a tall man, neither young nor old, for by the art of Aranloth, that lore of the Letharn which he had mastered, the form of the dead man was preserved. And the king's face, serene and kindly, was untouched by death or time.

The room was burdened by a weight of history. The very air, filled with fragrances that he well remembered from those other faraway tombs, those spices and resins and oils that preserved and freshened, smelled sweet.

He gazed at the king, and reverence overcame him. He knelt and bowed his head. Partly in near-worship of a legend, partly in awe of a man. He was not surprised to sense the Lindrath to his left, and Erlissa to his right, do the same.

He did not know why. Perhaps fate put the words in his mouth. Perhaps chance only. Perhaps forces ran through him that no man understood or named. But he voiced the Raithlin creed.

Our duty is to serve and protect
Our honor is to fight but not hate
Our love is for all that is good in the world

Out of the void, an answer came:

Well did you serve and protect

180

High was your honor, low was your hate
Your love for good was a beacon of light

Lanrik knew those words. Mourners recited them at the funeral of every Raithlin.

He looked up. Conhain stared at him. Not with the eyes of a dead man, nor yet the eyes of the living, but by enchantment that transcended life and death.

The king rose on his bier. His stately robes, silken things, sown with gold thread and studded by rare gems, whispered as he moved. Silver bands gleamed on wrists and forearms. A gold torc glittered around his neck, and a mighty sword hung from his side.

Conhain paused, and then like a young man, he swung himself over the side of the marble bier and vaulted to the floor. There he stood and gazed at the three of them.

Lanrik no longer knew if Conhain was alive or dead. He did not understand if this was a preserved body, a spirit, or some phantom of his mind that rose and stood before him. But the king's voice sounded real.

"Solemn words, and I have uttered them more than once. For I too was a Raithlin. I, who roamed the forests of the Halathrin and learned deeply of their lore. I was the first Raithlin, and the first Lindrath, and you have brought back memories that long have slept."

The king paused. His kind but sorrow-laden eyes studied them.

"Solemn words, but few others could rouse me. But this is no Raithlin initiation ceremony, nor even a funeral."

Lanrik swayed to his feet. The others did likewise. They stepped back. A sense of awe threatened to overcome them. And if not that, then dread, for the living had no place conversing with the dead.

Conhain did not move. "Do not fear me. I have not woken to cause harm, but to help. For assuredly, help is needed. This is the foretold hour when Ebona sits on the throne of Esgallien. It burdens me, though long I knew the day would come, and long I waited for it, and for you."

The king's eyes glittered in the light of Erlissa's staff. Lanrik spoke. His voice seemed harsh and thick.

"My King? You have waited for *us*?"

"I waited for *you*."

Lanrik did not know what to say.

"Show me your sword," the king commanded.

Lanrik lifted up the blade that he had taken from the captain. Conhain took hold of it. He glanced at it with puzzlement, and then cast it back into the anteroom.

"A poor sword," he said. "A poor sword indeed, and one that has drunk of the blood of innocents in service to Ebona's lust for death. It is not yours. Have you not another?"

Lanrik thought of his knives, and was about to pull one of them, but then realized that was not what Conhain meant.

"I've lost my Raithlin sword. But I have another. It lies safe in the fortress of Lòrenta."

"Describe it."

"It's a shazrahad blade, and I must keep it from the king. At least, so runs the prophecy."

Conhain laughed. It was a strange sound, deep in the dark, the laughter of the dead. It was full of the joy of life and kindness.

"Prophecies are odd things," he said. "I know it. I know much. The dead know many things."

Lanrik looked at him. This was not a moment to speak, even if awe did not make his tongue awkward.

182

"Have you not wondered why the prophecy of Assurah gathers pace? Have you not wondered why the sword ever draws danger and trouble? Aranloth has."

Lanrik shook his head. "I don't know, My Lord."

"Think on this, then."

The king straightened. Tall he stood, and solemn, until he appeared as his likeness carved into the towers that guarded Esgallien's gates.

"Long have I waited. Long have I dreamed amid the shoreless void. And I knew that moment, that one single moment amid the great dark, when first you laid hand upon the hilt of the sword. I felt prophecy waken. It stirred with life. You are no king, nor shall ever be, but you are of my line. Some of your forefathers wore Esgallien's crown. Your blood kindles the prophecy, but does not bring it to full vigor, which is both blessing and curse."

Lanrik stood in shock. He felt the heavy gaze of the Lindrath and Erlissa upon him. And yet what Conhain said made sense, and the dead did not lie. All of a sudden he understood Aranloth's many frowns and his uncertainty and hesitation about the sword, so strange when otherwise he was decisive.

The king surprised him anew.

"I have a gift," Conhain said.

Lanrik felt his heart flutter. He dare not consider what the long dead might think fit to bestow to the living. It too might be both blessing and curse. But he inclined his head and waited.

"You need a sword. A sword fit for one of my line. One day the city will fall. My sword, the sword I now give unto you, will be needed then, and in the days that follow. Take it out of the dark, take it into the light, that it may help those who most need it."

The king drew the great blade that hung at his side. Fable told that the Halathrin forged it. It was long. It glittered in the dark. And it held power. Some force was in it, some force that preserved, for no blemish was upon it. The leather-wrapped hilt remained soft, and the blade shone with an inner light.

The king turned it in his hand. For a moment, he tested its weight, felt some stirring of memory or life, and then he handed it, hilt first, to Lanrik.

It filled the air between them, a thing of legend and power, and Lanrik hesitated.

"Take it," the king commanded.

Lanrik took it. His hands trembled.

Conhain removed his belt and sheath, and passed them to him.

"Put it on."

Lanrik fumbled with the belt, but Erlissa helped him. It fitted well. The sword of Conhain hung at his side.

He looked up at the tall king. "Is there no hope for Esgallien? Is it true, that nothing lasts forever? Not men, nor chiefs ... nor even cities?"

Conhain gazed at him. His kindly eyes filled with sorrow, and for a moment he appeared as Aranloth so often did.

"It is true."

"How then can I fight fate, even with such a gift?"

Conhain's gaze did not waver. "You cannot. My words were valid. But there is another truth, equally valid. Nothing lasts forever, but likewise, nothing is erased. No kind act, no brave deed, no sacrifice for love is ever expunged or made as though it never happened. Not death, nor the oblivion of the ages, nor the failing memory of a race can ever take it away or make it as though it never was. Remember that. Remember that all you now know and love was born of ruin and despair in

184

my time. Remember me. For I am your forefather, and I am proud of you."

The king began to fade, or Lanrik's vision to blur. Conhain stepped back to the bier and lay down. The light of Erlissa's staff flickered and leaped. A cold wind blew.

The king lay still upon the marble slab. The Red Cloth of Victory fluttered above him. Lanrik felt the sudden weight of Conhain's sword that hung now at his own side.

"We must go," Erlissa whispered. "Time runs swiftly. The Witch-queen will have felt the power that seethes here. She will hasten to investigate, and we must be gone."

Lanrik looked at the king. Tears rolled down his cheeks. He did not move.

17. In the Name of the King

Lanrik felt Erlissa tug at his arm, but it was only when the Lindrath pushed him that he began to move.

He stumbled into the antechamber, and then a few moments later into the next room. He did not see how Erlissa closed the doors behind them, but he heard them come too and saw a flash of light each time.

They reached the stairs that ascended into the park.

"Was it a dream?" he asked.

"I don't know," Erlissa answered. "But dream or no, the sword is real."

Lanrik put a hand to its hilt. It felt reassuring to his touch.

"We can sort all that out later," the Lindrath said. "For now, keep behind me, and walk quietly."

The Lindrath moved up the stairs. Erlissa followed, and Lanrik trailed behind. They did not know who, if anyone, might be up in the park, and that helped clear his mind. It was time to be a Raithlin again.

They made no noise, and when they reached the entrance, the Lindrath paused. From deep in the shadows he watched and waited. Evidently, he neither saw nor sensed anything out of place, for after a while he stepped forward onto the stone floor of the monument.

It was dark. The lights of the city glimmered in the distance. Of the captain and soldiers, there was no sign. What the man would do, Lanrik could not guess. As a captain in the Royal Guard, he answered to Ebona, and yet no man would want to tell her of such a failure. He might try to disappear into the city, just as the soldiers.

The park lay below them, fields and groves of shadow where enemies might lurk, but he saw nothing that worried him.

Erlissa sealed the tomb, triggering the lòhrengai that moved and concealed the door. After a momentary flash of light, and a deep thrumming in the stone beneath their feet, they walked to the edge of the monument. The verge of the grassed slope, and the statue in the stone-lined pond, were just ahead.

"Where to?" the Lindrath asked.

"The tor," Lanrik replied. "That's where we're meeting Aranloth, and where we'll figure out how to overthrow the Witch-queen."

The Lindrath hesitated. "I had not thought to leave the city … but if you want me, I'll come as well."

"Oh, we want you," Erlissa said. "You know more of Esgallien and how things stand in it than we could have discovered in months. With you, our quest is more than successful."

Lanrik nodded. "But getting to the tor might not be easy. I had hoped to escape the park and the ring of sentries without a fight, but if you think the Witch-queen is coming, we'll have no time for subterfuge."

"She's coming," Erlissa said with certainty.

"Then we'd better go straight to the Hainer Lon, near where we entered, for that's the quickest route out of the city."

It was silent as they stepped onto the grass, but the quiet did not last. Even as they began to move, out from a grove of trees rode several men.

"Royal Guards!" the Lindrath said.

But that was not all. Something shambled beside the riders. It flickered with fire amid the dark, and the grass withered and smoked beneath its steps. The charred-man had come also.

187

"Behind me!" shouted Erlissa.

Both Lanrik and the Lindrath ignored her. They might not command magic to fight the charred-man, but they would not allow Erlissa to take the full brunt of its assault. They spread out to either side, swords drawn.

Lanrik felt the thrill of battle course through his body, and Conhain's blade was bright in the shadowy air.

The riders hung back. There were five of them, and Lanrik thought one of them was Brinhain. It would be no surprise. But he focused his attention on the charred-man.

The creature twitched and shuddered. It seemed feverish, as though unable to contain some great emotion. Perhaps it knew that its moment had come, that it could now fulfil the purpose Ebona had burdened it with. For surely its prey could not flee. Not on foot, with riders who could surround them in the open park, and herd them back toward it.

The charred-man headed for Erlissa. She stood her ground, unmoving despite the threat, seemingly content to wait and allow it to attack.

It lurched forward. Smoke curled up from the shriveled grass. An acrid scent burned in the air. The thing slowed, came to a standstill, and observed her. What thoughts crossed its mind, Lanrik did not know. For what it waited, he could not guess. But it did not pause long. One moment it stood still, and then the next it shuddered. Flame seethed around it, and it punched forward with a blistered fist.

A bolt of yellow-red flame sizzled through the air. It streaked to Erlissa. At the last moment, she raised her staff and blue light formed a shield before her. The bolt struck it. Fire writhed and twisted over the blue surface, and then fell down to the ground like water from the side of a building.

Erlissa made no further move. What her strategy was, Lanrik could not tell. But he was done waiting. Both he and the Lindrath, whether by the same instincts or similar training, moved toward it. They each drew knives and flung them as they approached.

The blades struck the creature. It staggered back a pace, and then straightened. With some care, it plucked the knives from its flesh; one from its throat, the other its belly. It held them before it. Its hands burned with fire, and steel began to smolder. The knives glowed red, and then turned white-hot.

The charred-man flung the first blade back at the Lindrath. White fire streaked through the air. The Lindrath dived and rolled, the blade hurtling into the ground near him and sparking into a thousand fragments.

The creature turned on him, and Lanrik waited until it flung his own knife back, and then he dived. It was a close thing. He felt fiery heat as it passed through the air near him, and then he was running at his attacker, Conhain's sword in his hand. From the corner of his eye he saw that the Lindrath did the same.

They never reached it. From behind the charred-man water tossed to and fro in the pond that held Conhain's statue. It coursed upward, infused with the blue light of Erlissa's lòhrengai. But though her power twisted through it, it was not lòhren-fire. The water swirled, became a spray, and then turned into roiling flurries of snow.

A blue-white cloud rolled over the charred-man. The creature lurched toward Erlissa. It shuddered, just as it had before. Fire curled outward from its body, but it did not escape the swirling blanket of snow. The flames stuttered out.

The charred-man fell to its knees. It opened its mouth to scream. No sound came, but the blue-white snow drove into its gaping maw. It convulsed. Steam rose from it, fogging the charged air.

For a moment, the gruesome sight remained unchanged. And then the snow was gone. The creature convulsed, let out a moan of great pain, the first noise that Lanrik had heard it utter, and then fire shot up harmlessly into the night sky and a putrid stench filled the air. The charred-man died and became what it always had been: the ruined body of a man, blackened and blistered.

Lanrik did not hesitate. He ran straight for Brinhain. The captain appeared shocked, but then kicked his horse into a gallop and charged.

The horse gathered speed, and Lanrik dived and rolled. Deadly hooves flew near him. Dirt and grass sprayed in his face. He twisted clear and came to his feet, just in time to see the Lindrath, older man though he was, leap across the horse's withers and tackle Brinhain.

They both fell heavily to the ground. The other guards galloped toward them, but a spray of lòhren-fire from Erlissa's staff sent them scrambling back.

The Lindrath rose, sword in hand. Brinhain did the same. But blade never touched blade.

"Wait!" cried Lanrik. "Stand back!"

The two men looked at him, and he approached. He turned to the captain.

"Enough is enough. The Witch-queen is evil, and she has only brought bloodshed to Esgallien. Will you not reconsider? Why fight for her?"

Brinhain did not hesitate. "Because she is power. Pure power. And because she'll defeat you."

"No, she won't. Her power was broken once before. You know the legends. We'll break it again."

190

"I've picked my side. I've picked the side that'll win. I'm pledged to her, and she rewards me. Surrender now, and perhaps she'll show you mercy."

"You won't reject her?"

"No. Never. At least," said Brinhain with a cold smile, "not so long as she's winning."

"Then you're a fool." He turned to the Lindrath. "This is personal. He struck Erlissa at the Bridge Inn. If there has to be a fight, it'll be me and him."

"So be it," said Brinhain. "I know your reputation, but I think it's overrated. I saw the way you backed down after I hit her."

Lanrik did not answer. Prudence had governed his actions at the inn, not fear.

He stepped forward. Conhain's sword glittered in the air. Brinhain wove his own blade in easy loops before him.

Lanrik knew he must win this battle quickly. There were soldiers all around the park. The Witch-queen was coming, and already they had been delayed too long. And yet he did not know how good Brinhain was. He was not one of the newly recruited Royal Guards, that much was clear. And a quick glance at his men showed that they were not worried. They appeared in good spirits, and seemed assured of the outcome. Perhaps they had never seen their captain defeated. If so, there was a first time for everything.

Lanrik lunged forward. He struck with speed and power, but it was only a feint. No sooner did he appear to commit to the blow, than he stepped to the side and away.

Brinhain's blade did not waver, and the man barely moved. It was a sign of skill. Of great skill, for he had either read Lanrik's intention, or discerned it during the lunge. Either way, he was good.

A moment later, Brinhain attacked. He drove forward, steel flying through the air in a blistering series of lightning strokes. His men cheered. Erlissa gasped, and the Lindrath remained silent.

Lanrik retreated. He moved back, but never in a straight or predictable line. Conhain's sword moved easily in his hand, parrying and deflecting. The attack could not continue long, for no one could move with such speed and power without exhausting themselves quickly.

After a few moments Brinhain ceased.

Lanrik looked at him calmly. "Is that all you've got?"

Brinhain went red. Rage contorted his face. He struck again, driving forward in uncontrolled anger.

Once more, Lanrik retreated. He made no move that he did not have to, rather, he preserved his strength and breathed deep of the nighttime air.

After a little while, he noticed that Brinhain's own breathing was ragged. He gulped in air, and his sword strokes slowed. At that point. Lanrik launched his own series of attacks.

Conhain's sword sang through the air. The ring of steel on steel peeled out into the park like jumbled bells, and his blade flashed as he drove forward.

Now, Brinhain retreated. He showed no limp from the gout that he suffered, for either the condition had improved or fear made him forget pain. He stepped back, but then tried to turn defense into attack by deflecting and lunging forward.

The point of his sword flicked across Lanrik's chest, but there was no force in the blow. The stroke was at the limit of Brinhain's reach, and his momentum was not fully committed. Lanrik, on the other hand, drove forward. With a smooth stroke he broke through the other's defenses. His blade hurtled at Brinhain's neck.

One moment it cut through the air, and the next he tilted his wrist so that the flat of it cracked into bone.

Brinhain reeled. He dropped his sword, and then he collapsed to the ground and lay still. He was not dead, though death he had deserved.

A moment Lanrik stood above his fallen enemy, wondering if he was wrong to spare him, but a moment only. The thunder of hooves over turf made him spin and face the other guards in a fighting crouch.

He need not have. Before they reached him, Erlissa flung up a wall of flame ahead of the horses, and the animals reared in sudden fright.

Three of the riders fell. Lanrik leaped over the flame and pulled the fourth from his saddle, throwing him to the ground.

"Run!" he yelled at the guards. "Or wither in flame!"

Erlissa could never make good on such a threat, but the men did not hesitate. They scrambled to their feet and dashed away. Only one lingered, looking as though he might fight, but as his comrades raced off, that thought left his mind.

The flame died. Lanrik quietened a horse, and took its bridle. The Lindrath was there also, his calm presence quieting another horse, and then Erlissa gathered in the reins of Brinhain's.

They leaped into the saddles.

"You just can't help yourself," Erlissa said with a laugh.

The Lindrath looked confused, and Lanrik flashed him a grin.

"I've had cause to steal horses … basically ever since the first time I met her."

"These aren't like the alar mounts that you took from the shazrahad though."

193

"No. Nothing in Esgallien is of that quality, but let's put them to the test anyway. It's time to ride."

He nudged his mount into a gallop, and the others followed. They headed over the dewy grass toward the Hainer Lon. Conhain's tomb was behind them, their own deaths somewhere ahead. He would do his best to ensure they did not find them soon.

They sped through the park. Turf flew behind them. The night air was cooling, and the horses seemed near fresh. They soon came to the soldiers. Beyond the picket line was the road, and safety, if they could reach it and then race to River Gate. Once there, they were out of the city, and between him and the Lindrath, no pursuit would find them. But they must get there first.

The picket line moved and shuffled. Lanrik had no desire to fight them, for they were just following orders. A commotion appeared somewhere to their left and out of his sight. Many soldiers took their gaze off the riders, but Lanrik could not understand why.

They galloped toward them. Few men, soldiers or otherwise, would hold their ground in the face of charging horses. Yet the men were many, and though caught by confusion, their role was simple and they understood it: stop anybody escaping the park.

The soldiers drew their swords, and Lanrik was doubtful of the horses. They belonged to the Royal Guard, and though they were good animals, he did not know their background. They might not be trained for this, and there was a risk that they would shy when close to the line. And that moment was coming soon.

He bent low over his mount, and drew his own sword. Nearby, the Lindrath did the same. He saw also that light flickered at the tip of Erlissa's staff.

The faces of the soldiers came into view, and as they did so he saw their expressions change. Resolve gave way to fear, and then surprise. Awe followed.

The men dropped their weapons and broke rank. A gap opened. Lanrik could not understand what was happening, and he glanced at the Lindrath. The Lindrath was looking behind him, and Lanrik followed his gaze. At last, he understood.

There were no longer just three riders. A fourth was fast catching up. But it was no ordinary rider, and the horse was like nothing that he had ever seen, at least in the flesh. It was roan colored, and massive. The noise of its hooves was as thunder. Upon its back was a mighty warrior; nay, a king. And not any king, but Conhain himself. Crowned was his head, and in his hand he held the Red Cloth of Victory. Whether illusion, or ghost, none born in Esgallien could fail to recognize him.

Wind whistled past Lanrik's ears. He passed through the gap. Soldiers nearby reeled away, and none made a stroke, and none shot with bow, though archers stood scattered among them. They all stared, open mouthed and wide eyed, and then suddenly a cry went up.

"Conhain! Conhain!"

Lanrik felt their jubilation. "The king returns!" he yelled, and many soldiers dropped to their knees.

One moment he rode on grass, and the next iron-shod hooves clattered on cobbles. Erlissa and the Lindrath raced beside him.

They turned to the right, heading toward River Gate. Just as they did so, Lanrik saw Ebona. She stood away to the left, next to a black carriage. Red fire dripped from her fingers. But her face was white, paler even than the dress she wore, and her eyes were deep pools of fear and doubt.

They sped away, but Lanrik yelled over his shoulder.

195

"The king returns! Down with the Witch-queen!" It was both threat and promise, and it would spread throughout the city.

They raced on. The great warhorse, Conhain upon his back, came with them. All through the city they galloped. Men saw them. Women saw them. Children saw them. Shouts of *Conhain! Conhain!* followed in their wake.

They came to River Gate in a rush, and then reined their mounts to a stop.

"Open! I am the Lindrath, and I command you in the name of the king!"

The soldiers did not hesitate. They opened the gate with trembling hands. Two ghosts were before them: Conhain and the Lindrath. Both were supposed to be dead, and word of the Witch-queen's subterfuge with the body at the palace would spread through the city and undermine her. She would now seem weak, and the people would know that resistance against her was possible.

In moments they rode free. They galloped down the road, grand estates to either side. The land was open, the way ahead clear. Behind them came no pursuit.

Lanrik glanced back one final time. The fourth rider was gone, but the last rumbling gait of a great warhorse could still be heard. Whether it was all just an apparition sprung from Erlissa's lòhrengai, or the ghost of Conhain, he did not know. But his heart sang with joy.

They rode toward Esgallien Ford. After that would come the tor, Aranloth, and then the overthrow of Ebona.

At least, so he hoped.

Epilogue

The moon rose like a silver ball in the dark sky. It seemed so large, so close, that Lanrik felt as though he could reach out from atop his place on the tor and pluck it from the sky.

Moonlight flowed over the shadowy grasslands below. He smelled dew on grass, the odor of stagnant swamps, and the cool fresh air of wind-swept Galenthern.

From the shadow-haunted swamps came a call that he knew well, the drawn out bellow of an aurochs, and from miles away in the silvery dark, the answer of another beast.

Lanrik was home. Home as even Esgallien City was not, and could never be. Behind him was Lathmai's cairn. There, a part of his heart always rested. Her sword remained untouched. It jutted up, just as he had set it in the rocks long ago. And her grave was tended. The Raithlin hiding on the plains grew wild flowers around it.

His brothers and sisters were here now, at the base of the tor, near two dozen of them. And the Lindrath was among them.

But that was only a part of why he felt at home. He glanced to his side. Erlissa stood there. She leaned on her walnut staff, in that same pose that he had seen Aranloth take so many times. If he was home, it was because she was near. When he stood next to her, sensed her presence, he felt as though all was right in the world. Home was wherever she was.

The moon rose higher. It floated in the heavens above the shadowy sea that was green-grassed Galenthern, and he felt the first tug of doubt. Aranloth had said to meet him here, on the full moon, and the lòhren was late. It was not like him.

He looked at Erlissa. She too sensed it. He read it on her face.

"Where is he?" Lanrik asked.

Erlissa did not answer. Her gaze passed over Galenthern, sweeping over grass, out beyond grasslands and swamps. He wondered if her lòhren-senses flew so far as the Graèglin Dennath, where Aranloth had gone.

A long time she looked. A long time she remained motionless. The moon rose higher. Lanrik's uneasiness deepened.

"He does not come," Erlissa said.

"Why?"

She turned to him. She appeared pale and tired, and yet there was a light of anger on her face.

"He cannot. The enemy has him."

Thus ends *Courage of the Conquered*. The Raithlindrath series continues in book four, *Blades of the Banished*. Once again, Lanrik and Erlissa are caught up in events destined to shape the future of the land.

Sign up below and be the first to hear about new book releases, see previews and learn of upcoming discounts. http://eepurl.com/Rswv1

Visit my website at www.homeofhighfantasy.com

Encyclopedic Glossary

Many races dwell in Alithoras. All have their own language, and though sometimes related to one another, the changes sparked by migration, isolation and various influences often render these tongues unintelligible to each other.

The ascendancy of Halathrin culture, combined with their widespread efforts to secure and maintain allies against elug incursions, has made their language the primary means of communication between diverse peoples.

For instance, a soldier of Esgallien addressing a ship's captain from Camarelon would speak Halathrin, or a simplified version of it, even though their native speeches stem from the same ancestral language.

This glossary contains a range of names and terms. Many are of Halathrin origin, and their meaning is provided. The remainder derive from native tongues and are obscure, so meanings are only given intermittently.

Some variation exists within the Halathrin language, chiefly between the regions of Halathar and Alonin. The most obvious example is the latter's preference for a "dh" spelling instead of "th".

Often, Camar names and Halathrin elements are combined. This is especially so for the aristocracy. No other tribes had such long-term friendship with the

Halathrin, and though in this relationship they lost some of their natural culture, they gained nobility and knowledge in return.

List of abbreviations:

Azn. Azan

Cam. Camar

Chg. Cheng

Comb. Combined

Cor. Corrupted form

Duth. Duthenor

Esg. Esgallien

Hal. Halathrin

Leth. Letharn

Prn. Pronounced

Alar: *Azn.* A strain of horses raised in the southern deserts of Alithoras. Bred for endurance, but capable of bursts of speed. Most valued possession of the Azan people, who measure wealth and status by their number. In their culture, where a person on foot is likely to die between water sources, horse-theft is punished by torture and death.

Alithoras: *Hal.* "Silver land." The Halathrin name for the continent they settled after the exodus. Refers to the extensive river and lake systems they found and their appreciation of the beauty of the land.

Angle: The land hemmed in by the Carist Nien and Erenian rivers, especially the area in proximity to their divergence. Once the homeland of the Letharn people. Their empire is gone, but the tombs of their dead remain.

Aranloth: *Hal.* "Noble might." A lòhren.

Assurah: *Azn.* A renowned sword-smith of ancient Azanbulzibar, capital city of the Azan people. He was also adept at elùgai, and his work was sought by the rich and powerful of many nations.

Aurochs: The wild forebear of domesticated cattle. They are larger and more aggressive than their tamed descendants and prefer to graze and forage in swamps and wet forests. The "s" at the end of their name is both singular and plural.

Azan: *Azn.* Desert-dwelling people. Their nobility often serve as leaders of elug armies. They are a prideful race, often haughty and domineering, but they also adhere to a strict code of honor.

Bragga Mor: *Cam.* A great poet and storyteller of Esgallien. He traces his ancestry back to the days when one of his forefathers served Conhain as both bodyguard and court bard. Historians dispute this, but Bragga pays them no heed.

Bridge Inn: An inn beyond Esgallien's northern wall. Named after the nearby bridge that spans Esgallien Creek.

Brinhain: *Comb. Esg & Hal.* First element unknown, second "hero." A captain in Esgallien's Royal Guard.

Caladhrist: *Hal. Prn.* Kal-ath-rist. "Gold gorge." A valley north of Esgallien. Rich in gold and the source of much of the city's wealth subsequent to the depletion of closer alluvial deposits. Many others mined the valley through the history of Alithoras, including the Letharn. A dangerous place and believed by many to be haunted.

Camar: *Cam. Prn.* Kay-mar. A race of interrelated tribes that migrated in two main stages. The first brought them to the vicinity of Halathar; in the second, they separated and established cities along a broad sweep of eastern Alithoras.

Camarelon: *Cam. Prn.* Kam-arelon. A port city and capital of a Camar tribe. It was founded after Esgallien as the waves of migrating people settled the more southerly lands first. Each new migration tended northward. It is perhaps the most representative of a traditional Camar realm, while Esgallien is the most influenced by Halathrin culture.

Cardoroth: *Cor. Hal. Comb. Cam.* A Camar city, often called Red Cardoroth. Some say this alludes to the red granite commonly used in the construction of its buildings, others that it refers to a prophecy of destruction.

Careth Nien: *Hal. Prn.* Kareth nyen. "Great River." Largest river in Alithoras. Has its source in the mountains of Anast Dennath and runs southeast across the land before emptying into the sea. It was over this river (which sometimes freezes along its northern length) that the Camar, Duthenor and other tribes migrated into the eastern lands.

Careth Tar: *Cor. Hal.* "Careth Tar(an) – Great Father." Title of respect for the leader of the lòhrens.

Carist Nien: *Hal.* "Ice River." A river of northern Alithoras that has its source in the hills of Lòrenta.

Caracas: *Hal.* "Red knife." A member of Esgallien's Royal Guard.

Carnona: *Cam.* The Guardian of Enorìen. A creature of ùhrengai who has remained in her birthing lands.

Carnyx: The sacred horn of Conhain's people and related tribes. An instrument of brass, man high with a mouth fashioned in the likeness of a fierce animal, often a boar or bear. Winded in battle and designed to intimidate the foe with its otherworldly sound. Some believe it invokes supernatural aid.

City Watch: A branch of the army used by the rulers of Esgallien to maintain civil order and to investigate, and deter, crime.

Conhain: *Comb. Esg & Hal.* First element unknown, second "hero." Accounted the first king of Esgallien.

Conhain Court: The heart of Esgallien city. A large square, colonnaded on all sides, and containing bronze statues of all Esgallien's kings and queens.

Conhain's Rest: A park in Esgallien. One of many places said to be the site of Conhain's burial.

Ebona: *Cam.* A witch. A being of ùhrengai who has long since left her birthing lands.

Eleth nar duril: *Hal.* "lie in peace." A phrase from Halathrin funerary rites.

Elùgai: *Hal. Prn.* Eloo-guy. "Shadowed force." The sorcery of an elùgroth.

Elùgroth: *Hal. Prn.* Eloo-groth. "Shadowed horror." A sorcerer.

Elugs: *Hal.* "That which creeps in shadows." A cruel and superstitious race that inhabits the southern lands, especially the Graèglin Dennath.

Elù-Randùr: *Hal.* "Blade of the Shadow." An elùgroth leader. Formerly a lòhren.

Enorìen: *Cam.* The Eastern Hills. A land where ùhrengai runs strong. Protected by the Guardian Carnona.

Erlissa: *Esg.* A young woman of Esgallien. Also known as the Seeker. Now a lòhren.

Esgallien: *Hal. Prn.* Ez-gally-en. A city established by King Conhain. Named after the nearby ford.

Esgallien Ford: *Hal.* "Es – rushing water, gal(en) – green, lien – to cross: place of the crossing onto the green plains." A ford of the Careth Nien.

Exodus: The arrival of the Halathrin into Alithoras from an outside land. They came by ship and beached north of Anast Dennath.

Faramond: *Comb. Hal & Esg.* First element "to shear, cut or divide." Second element "A hoard, especially one guarded by a dragon."

Foresight: Premonition of the future. Can occur at random as a single image or as a longer sequence of events. Can also be deliberately sought by entering the realm between life and death where the spirit is released from the body to travel through space and time. To achieve this, the body must be brought to the very threshold of death. The first method is uncontrollable and rare. The second exceedingly rare but controllable for those with the skill and willingness to endure the danger.

Founding: The arrival of Conhain and his people near Esgallien Ford. This was nine hundred and fifty three years ago at the time of Lanrik's meeting with Erlissa and Aranloth.

Free cities: A group of cooperative city states that pool military resources to defend themselves against attack. Founded prior to Esgallien. Initially ruled by kings and queens, now by a senate.

Galenthern: *Hal.* "Green flat." Southern plains bounded by the Careth Nien and the Graèglin Dennath mountain range.

Gilhain: *Comb. Esg & Hal.* First element unknown, second "hero." A Raithlin.

Graèglin Dennath: *Hal. Prn.* Greg-lin dennath. "Mountains of ash." Chain of mountains in southern Alithoras. The landscape is one of jagged stone and boulder, relieved only by gaping fissures from which plumes of ashen smoke ascend, thus leading to its name. Believed to be impassable because of the danger of poisonous air flowing from cracks, and the ground unexpectedly giving way, swallowing any who dare to tread its forbidden paths. In other places swathes of molten stone run in rivers down its slopes.

Great North Road: An ancient construction of the Halathrin. Built at a time when they had settlements in the northern reaches of Alithoras. Warriors traveled swiftly from north to south in order to aid the main population who dwelt in Halathar when they faced attack from the south.

Guardian: A creature of sentient ùhrengai that preserves its birthing land.

Gwalchmur: *Esg.* A former Raithlin of Esgallien.

Hainer Lon: *Hal. Prn.* Hiner lon. "Heroes way." The main thoroughfare of Esgallien.

Hakalakadan: *Azn.* A revered title among the Azan peoples.

Halathar: *Hal.* "Dwelling place of the people of Halath." The forest realm of the Halathrin.

Halathgar: *Hal.* "Bright Star." Actually a constellation. Also known as the Lost Huntress.

Halathrin: *Hal.* "People of Halath." A race named after a mighty lord who led an exodus of his people to the continent of Alithoras in pursuit of justice, having sworn to redress a great evil. They are human, though of fairer form, greater skill and higher culture. They possess an inherent unity of body, mind and spirit enabling insight and endurance beyond other races of Alithoras. Reported to be immortal, but killed in great numbers during their conflicts with the evil they seek to destroy.

Halls of Lore: Library of records maintained by lòhrens of the history, knowledge and wisdom of the nations of Alithoras. Accumulated over millennia and one of the treasures of Lòrenta.

Hamalath: *Hal.* "Sorrow joy". An open-air theatre where dramas of history, tragedy and humor are conducted. Derived from the Halathrin who built many. In Esgallien called simply "The Hamalath," as there is only one of significant size.

Harakgar: *Leth.* The three sisters. Creatures of ùhrengai brought into being by the lore of the Letharn. Their purpose is to protect the tombs of their creators from robbery.

Haranast: *Hal.* "Horse race." A racetrack. Its form was derived from the Halathrin but the love of horseracing by the Camar predates the exodus of the immortals. A successful rider, or horse, could be more famous and better loved than tribal chiefs or kings. The stealing of a racehorse is punishable by death.

Karlenthern: *Hal.* "Games field." The location of many events during the Spring Games and other athletic competitions during the year.

Lake Alithorin: *Hal.* "Silver lake." A lake of northern Alithoras.

Lanrik: *Esg.* A Raithlin. Also called the Raithlindrath.

Lathmai: *Comb. Hal. & Esg.* "Joy and unknown element." A Raithlin. She was killed in service to her country.

Letharn: *Hal.* "Stone Raisers. Builders." A race of people that in antiquity ruled much of Alithoras. Only traces of their civilization remain.

Lindrath: *Hal.* "People lord." A shortening of Raithlindrath. Commander of the Raithlin organization.

Lòhren: *Hal. Prn.* Ler-ren. "Knowledge giver – a counselor." Other terms used by various nations include wizard, druid and sage.

Lòhren-fire: A defensive manifestation of lòhrengai. The color of the flame varies according to the skill and temperament of the lòhren.

Lòhrengai: *Hal. Prn.* Ler-ren-guy. "Lòhren force." Enchantment, spell or use of arcane power. A manipulation and transformation ùhrengai, the natural energy inherent in all things. Each use takes something from the user. Likewise, some part of the transformed energy infuses them. Lòhrens use it sparingly.

Lòrenta: *Hal. Prn.* Ler-rent-a. "Hills of knowledge." Uplands in northern Alithoras in which the stronghold of the lòhrens is established.

Marik: A name assumed by Lanrik to conceal his true identity.

Mecklar: *Esg.* Was once a senior member of King Murhain's retinue. A traitor slain by Lanrik in single combat.

Merenloth: *Hal. Prn.* Mair-en-loth. "Words of power." A place for philosophical debate, reciting poetry and the chanting of bards. Derived from Halathrin practice. Often full to capacity during times of change. King Danhain, disguised as a bard, often frequented the Merenloth and chanted pre-founding lays passed down from his grandfather. After the performance he discoursed with the crowd to determine what the people thought of the king's rule. He sometimes changed his decisions after such debates.

Murhain: *Esg.* The current king of Esgallien. He was a younger son of the previous king and assumed the throne unexpectedly. Earlier in his life, he had attempted to train as a Raithlin but failed their vigorous standards.

Musraka: *Azn.* A shazrahad.

Otherworld: Esgallien term for a mingling of half-remembered history, myth and the spirit world.

Pattern-welded: A blade forged and reforged from bundles of iron rods that are twisted and beaten. This creates a flexible core to which a hard edge is added. The process produces superior, distinctive and sought-after weapons.

Portico: A covered colonnade, often at the front of a building.

Raithlin: *Hal.* "Range and report people." A scouting and saboteur organization. They derive from ancient contact with, and the teachings of, the Halathrin. Disbanded by the king of Esgallien, but founded anew by Lanrik and dedicated to the service of all Alithoras.

Raithlin motif: A trotting fox looking back over its shoulder. A half moon rides above the animal. Symbolizes cunning, stealth and boldness.

Raithlin crawl: A famous technique of stealth. It requires that the palms rest on the earth and the elbows remain tucked in to the body for support and silhouette reduction. The bodyweight is borne on the forearms and only one leg. The other is carefully brought forward in order to avoid making noise while moving.

Raithlin creed: "Our duty is to serve and protect. Our honor is to fight but not hate. Our love is for all that is good in the world."

Raithlin principles of concealment: The Raithlin believe the eye recognizes movement first, silhouette second and color last. Using these principles enables them to best determine how to remain unseen in varying circumstances.

Raithlindrath: *Hal.* "Lord of range and report people."

Red Cloth of Victory: The highest symbol of courage and determination in Esgallien society.

Rhodmai: *Esg.* An inn servant who married King Danhain and ruled as queen after his death. Her reign was noted for civic constructions and marked for its peace. So much so that a prosperous period for the city has ever since been known as "Rhodmai's Peace."

Royal Guard: Bodyguards to Esgallien royalty.

Shazrahad: *Azn.* The Azan who commands an elug army.

Shurilgar: *Hal.* "Midnight Star." An elùgroth. Also called the betrayer of nations.

Sorcerer: See elùgroth.

Spring Games: A series of athletic and skill-based competitions in Esgallien deriving from antiquity. Other Camar peoples also conduct the games, sometimes under a different name. Before the tribes diverged, they met at various sacred sites marked by standing stones. There, amid sporting games, feasting and trade, chiefs were chosen, disputes settled and ceremonies conducted.

Tamril: A name assumed by Erlissa to conceal her true identity.

Tombs of the Letharn: The ancient burial place of the Letharn people. All members of the population, throughout the course of their long civilization, were laid to rest here. It was believed that to be interred elsewhere was to condemn the spirit to a true death, rather than an afterlife. The dead were preserved, and returned even from the far reaches of the empire. This was withheld from perpetrators of treason and heinous crimes. These were buried in special cemeteries near the river. Petty criminals were afforded an opportunity to redeem their place in the tombs on payment of a fine determined by the head-priest.

Tor: A hill rising up from the plains of Galenthern. Site of Lathmai's grave.

Ùhrengai: *Hal. Prn.* Er-ren-guy. "Original force." The primordial force that existed before substance or time, light or dark, life or death, good or evil.

Witchery: A type of elùgai. Distinct from the common spell-craft and potion-making carried out by some village healers.

Witch-fire: A potent attack of elùgai.

Witch-queen: See Ebona.

From the author

I'm a man born in the wrong era. My heart yearns for faraway places and even further afield times. Tolkien had me at the beginning of *The Hobbit* when he said, ". . . one morning long ago in the quiet of the world . . ."

Sometimes I imagine myself in a Viking mead-hall. The long winter night presses in, but the shimmering embers of a log in the hearth hold back both cold and dark. The chieftain calls for a story, and I take a sip from my drinking horn and stand up . . .

Or maybe the desert stars shine bright and clear, obscured occasionally by wisps of smoke from burning camel dung. A dry gust of wind marches sand grains across our lonely campsite, and the wayfarers about me stir restlessly. I sip cool water and begin to speak.

I'm a storyteller. A man to paint a picture by the slow music of words. I like to bring faraway places and times to life, to make hearts yearn for something they can never have, unless for a passing moment.